U0572525

Summer
1925

马尔智蜜月日记

（一九二五年七月三日—八月四日）

谢小珮
张倩 译

图书在版编目（CIP）数据

马尔智蜜月日记/马尔智著；谢小玼，张倩译. —北京：中华书局，2016.10
ISBN 978-7-101-12134-6

Ⅰ.马…　Ⅱ.①马…②谢…③张…　Ⅲ.日记-作品集-美国-现代　Ⅳ.I712.65

中国版本图书馆 CIP 数据核字（2016）第 218556 号

书　　名	马尔智蜜月日记	
著　　者	马尔智	
译　　者	谢小玼　张　倩	
责任编辑	陈　虎	
出版发行	中华书局	
	（北京市丰台区太平桥西里 38 号　100073）	
	http://www.zhbc.com.cn	
	E-mail：zhbc@ zhbc.com.cn	
印　　刷	北京瑞古冠中印刷厂	
版　　次	2016 年 10 月北京第 1 版	
	2016 年 10 月北京第 1 次印刷	
规　　格	开本/710×1000 毫米　1/16	
	印张 10¼　插页 2　字数 100 千字	
印　　数	1-2600 册	
国际书号	ISBN 978-7-101-12134-6	
定　　价	98.00 元	

编委会

主　编：刘　颖

副主编：卓　军　杨小茹　阮少茜　章玉兰

翻　译：谢小珮　张　倩

校　译：阮少茜

前 言
Foreword

　　"天下西湖三十六，就中之最属杭州"，历史上杭州西湖以其"景致天成，宛如画图"的独特魅力风靡国内外。世界著名旅行家马可·波罗盛赞杭州为"最美丽华贵的天城"。2011年6月24日，在第35届世界遗产大会上，杭州西湖文化景观成功登录《世界遗产名录》，再次进入了西方的视野。这顶"世界遗产"的桂冠所具有的巨大吸引力，提高了西湖在国际上的地位，它的名望、美誉，使其成为最具特色之杭州文化。

　　"Of the country's thirty-six West Lakes, Hangzhou claims the best." For countless years, Hangzhou's West Lake has been known home and abroad for her "picturesque landscape". The world's renowned adventurer Marco Polo extolled Hangzhou as "the City of Heaven, the most beautiful and magnificent in the world." On June 24, 2011, during the 35th session of the World Heritage Committee, the West Lake Cultural Landscape of Hangzhou was inscribed into the World Heritage List, reprising her past glory in the West. The inscription has brought more attention to West Lake in the global context, further accentuating its reputation as the most featured cultural element of Hangzhou.

　　杭州西湖世界文化遗产监测管理中心承担着西湖文化景观的宣传、研究等工作。为进一步推动西湖融入国际文化潮流，使更多的世界友人了解珍贵的西湖文化遗产，更真切地体验西湖遗产的历史意义，我们希望通过拓宽国内外的信息渠道，发掘一切可利用的资源，尤其是与境外博物馆、图书馆以及档案资料室或高等院校等研究机构建立资源共享的关系，并采取出版物、展览、研讨会等并驾齐驱的学术形式，将传播西湖文化的研究推向纵深，为全世界展示一个天生丽质的"大家闺秀"——杭州西湖。一个偶然的机会，我们结识了美国史密斯松尼博物学院下属的佛利尔和萨克勒两亚洲博物馆的客座独立书画学人谢小珮。近些年来，谢小珮女士致力于构建一座我们与佛利尔博物馆之间的西湖文化桥梁，疏通了传递信息和宣传交流的途径。出于对传统文化的珍爱，和对西湖景致的钟情，她代替我们与佛利尔美术馆的视觉资料档案部的负责人戴维德先生联系了出版和展览的具体事宜，经过协商获得了对方的许可，最终为我们提供了佛利尔博物馆藏，原东亚艺术史专家本杰明·马尔智于 1925 年 7 月 4 日至 8 月 4 日间在杭州所拍摄的七十余张照片及他在杭州所记的三十七页日记，促成了这本书的出版，让世人有幸再见百年前充满神韵的杭城和风姿绰约的西湖。

The Monitoring and Management Center of Hangzhou West Lake World Cultural Heritage is working on the promotion and research of the West Lake Cultural Landscape. With the aim of furthering the fusion of the cultural elements of the heritage site into the globe's cultural context and encouraging better understanding of its value and historical significance, we endeavor to broaden the channels for information sharing, explore and employ all available resources, establish an information sharing mechanism with international partners, museums, libraries, archives, universities or research institutes, in particular, and stimulate research into West Lake and its related culture in the format of publication, exhibition and symposium. In this way, we will better showcase the breathtaking beauty of the West Lake. On one occasion, we met Sarah Shay, an independent Chinese calligraphy and painting scholar for the Freer Gallery of Art and Arthur M. Sackler Gallery of the Smithsonian Institution, who is interested in becoming a liaison to bridge the cultural exchange between the Freer Gallery of Art and us. In recent years, Sarah helped us greatly in promotion and communication of the West Lake culture, and as an enthusiast of Chinese traditional culture and an admirer of the picturesque West Lake, she has contacted David in charge of the visual archives of the Freer Gallery of Art for arrangements of publications and exhibitions. Her Endeavor has made available the 70 plus photos and 37 pages of diary created by Benjamin March, an expert of East Asia Art History, during his visit of Jangzhou from July 4th to August 4th, 1925.

我们将在此基础上，创立一个"西人眼里的西湖"的窗口，循着世人的向往，体察大众的趣味，诠释一个美好、浪漫、宜居的杭州。让西湖以其非凡的影响力在国际上广泛延伸。

In a similar context, we have created a perspective of the beautiful, romantic and highly livable Hangzhou that is friendly to westerners' mindset to widen the cultural gravitation of West Lake.

杨小茹

Yang Xiaoru

2016 年 5 月

May 2016

序
Preface

　　杭州，一个优雅又有着浪漫情怀的城市，从古至今传唱着多少才子佳人的爱情故事。人蛇共枕的白素贞与许仙、双宿双飞的梁山伯与祝英台，这些凄美的民间爱情传说，都将故事场景设定在了美丽的西子湖畔。出身于钱塘（今杭州）大族的清初戏曲家洪昇，在1688年完成了轰动一时的《长生殿》，着墨于唐玄宗、杨贵妃二人缠绵悱恻的爱情故事。作者浓墨熏染了西湖水之柔情，不顾当时的政治环境，谱写了一曲唯美的帝妃爱情传奇。水因情而变得愈发婀娜，情因水而变得愈发柔美，杭州也因此成为人人艳羡的"人间天堂"。

　　Hangzhou, elegant and romantic, has fostered numerous love stories since ancient times. The legends of Madame White Snake and Butterfly Lovers all took place at the picturesque West Lake. The Palace of Eternal Love, created in 1688 by Hong Sheng (an early Qing Dynasty playwright who was born of a famous clan in Hangzhou), depicts the beautiful yet tragic love story of Emperor Xuanzong of the Tang Dynasty and his favorite consort Lady Yang. Some would say the author had very possibly been inspired by the grace of West Lake to create this beautiful literary piece that was a sharp contrast to the harsh political environment then. These stories and literary figures add a romantic appeal to both West Lake and Hangzhou, a city known as the "paradise of the human realm".

　　"一片湖，一条江，一座山，这是一座得天独厚的城市。西湖边动人的婀娜，钱塘江边追寻的脚步，这是一座懂得将幸福拥揽入怀的城市。没有来这里总是遗憾，来到这里，却不得不离开，更是遗憾。"2009年最具幸福感城市颁奖晚会上，组委会对杭州这个既恢宏大气又不失柔美温润的城市如是说。幸福是什么？生活在这个城市里的每个人都有不同的理解。感性的女作家夏达说："杭州的幸福，就是细腻温润，气象万千，永远让人有惊喜。"思维缜密的谍战作家麦家说："我梦想过天堂的样子，就是杭州的样子。这个城市的幸福在于公益，比如遍布全城的公共自行车，这是一个为老百姓着想的城市。"习近平总书记更是在安塔利亚峰会上盛赞杭州"风景如画，堪称人间天堂"。

"With a lake, a river and a mountain, this is a city blessed by nature. From the striking beauty of West Lake to the tracing footprints cast on the Qiantang riverbank, the city knows how to embrace bliss. Rue rises for not being here, not more than plaints on departure." These were the comments the organizing committee made on this graceful and magnificent city at the 2009 Happiest City awarding ceremony. What is happiness? The answer varies for every person living in this city. Ms. Xia Da, a sensible writer said, "The happiness in Hangzhou lies in its refined glamour, dynamic and striking!" Mai Jia, a meticulous writer of spy thrillers, made his statement, "I have dreamed the Heavens as Hangzhou where the city's happiness is her public welfare, such as the public bikes you can find everywhere. A thoughtful city for her people."President Xi Jinping gave his praise to Hangzhou during the Antalya Summit, "A picturesque landscape and a paradise."

这片山水，一旦涉足其间，便被深深吸引。因为西湖，杭州成为历朝历代文人贤士"诗意的栖居地"。白居易、苏东坡、林和靖、岳飞、于谦……无论出世入世，抑或生生死死；无论思念，抑或是追随，西湖早已是根植于他们内心的"精神家园"。从13世纪意大利人马可·波罗赞赏杭州是"世界上最美丽华贵的天城"开始，吸引了大批来自异国他乡的游历者，他们怀揣好奇之心，意图一睹这座神秘城市的风采。17世纪同样来自意大利的卫匡国、20世纪初出生在杭州的司徒雷登，都将杭州作为自己的最后归宿地。

Visitors to the city are sure to be captivated by its beauty. Thanks to West Lake, Hangzhou was the source of poetic inspirations for scholars and the worthies of dynasties. West Lake remained the "spiritual home" that Bai

Juyi, Su Dongpo, Lin Hejing, Yue Fei, Yu Qian and many others yearned for or pursued throughout their lives, whether they were officials or commoners. The world's most beautiful and magnificent imperial city, extolled by Italian Marco Polo of the 13th century, has attracted flocks of foreign tourists with abundant curiosity to explore the mysterious exoticness of Hangzhou, which both Martino Martini, an Italian of the 17th century, and John Leighton Stuart, born in Hangzhou in the early 20th century took as their resting place.

同样受马可·波罗影响，90 年前的夏天 (1925 年)，西子湖畔，来自美国的马尔智夫妇这样诠释着自己的幸福：新婚燕尔，生活无忧，如胶似漆的相依相伴，度过了他们人生中最美妙的时光。他们一边醉心于绝美的湖光山色，一边享受着国人的尊崇礼遇。湖中泛舟、仲夏夜赏月、灵隐寺诵经、古城墙上寻古、孤山间探幽……他们携手几乎走遍了西湖的角角落落。7 月 30 日，是这对年轻夫妇结婚一个月的纪念日。这天，马尔智记录了当时的感受："今天是我们的第一个'满月'。结婚的这一个月，我们都甚感愉悦。"这一切对于马尔智来说，除了满足便是满意。在他离开杭州的那天，充满深情地写道："'上有天堂，下有苏杭。'还有什么地方能比杭州、苏州这些简直就是天堂的地方更适合度蜜月呢？"（1925 年 8 月 4 日）

Inspired by Marco Polo, in summer of 1925, 90 years ago, March and his newlywed wife from the US arrived at West Lake for their honeymoon, where they documented the happiness of their marriage and deep love of each other, the best time of their life. Captured by the stunning beauty of the natural landscape and Chinese hospitality, the couple explored every corner of the West Lake area. They boated on the lake, enjoyed summer moonlight, had their minds cleansed by the chanting in the Lingyin Temple, and visited the wall relics of the old city and the deep, tranquil mountains. On July 30, on the conclusion of the first month of their marriage, March wrote down his feelings, "Today is the first "full moon" of our marriage. Nothing can describe our joy." To March, the only thing besides satisfaction was contentment. On the day of their departure, March described so passionately, "With Heavens above, I am content with Suzhou and Hangzhou." No place else is made better for a honeymoon." (August 4, 1925)

马尔智 (Benjamin Franklin March，Jr.，1899—1934) 出身于基督教家庭，毕业于芝加哥大学，后在协和神学院进修一年，1923 年以美会传教士的身份派往中国河北大学（音译，Hopei university）任教。第一次踏上中国这片神秘的土地，马尔智便表现出了对东方古典艺术的热爱。经过几年的磨砺，马尔智逐渐成长为美国东亚艺术史研究领域的权威人士，此后陆续出版了《梅伶兰姿》（*ORCHID HAND PATTERNS OF MEI LAN-FANG*），《中国画的一些专业术语》（*SOME TECHNICAL TERMS OF CHINESE PAINTING*），《我们博物馆内的中国和日本》（*CHINA AND JAPAN IN OUR MUSEUMS*）等一些介绍及推广中国文化的专业书籍。经梅·约翰逊介绍，马尔智结识了跟随传教士父亲在南京定居的多萝西（Dorothy Rowe），并于 1925 年 6 月 30 日在南京完婚，随后踏上蜜月之旅。

Benjamin Franklin March, Jr. (1899 - 1934), born of a Christian family, graduated from the University of Chicago and studied one year at Union Theological Seminary. In 1923, assigned to teach as a US missionary in Hopei University (Hebei U.) of China, March stepped for the first time on the mysterious China, where he discovered his passion in the classical art of the East. After a few years, March became an authoritative figure of the East Asia art in the US. He published writings on Chinese culture, such as Orchid Hand Patterns of Mei Lan-Fang, Some Technical Terms of Chinese Painting, and China and Japan in Our Museums. Introduced by Mei Johnson, March and Dorothy Rowe, who lived in Nanjing with her missionary father met and married to each other in Nanjing on June 30, 1925. Soon, the couple began their honeymoon trip.

此次编译出版的《马尔智蜜月日记》，主要摘录了马尔智夫妇在杭州度蜜月的点点滴滴，时间为 1925 年 7 月 3 日至 8 月 4 日，共 33 天。

日记的大部分由马尔智先生完成，平铺直叙地记录了夫妇俩在西湖边、杭州城游历的经过，闪现着马尔智的智慧和思考。从 7 月 30 日开始，日记由妻子多萝西接手，文笔细腻，观察入微，从女性的视角为我们解读了 90 年前西湖的各种美好。

This edition of March's Honeymoon Diary is a collection of dribs and drabs of the couple's honeymoon between July 3 and August 4, 1925, a total of 33 days. The diary was mostly written by March about their stay and experience at West Lake and Hangzhou, recording March's wits and thoughts and Dorothy's fine detailed observations (from July 30) of the beauty of West Lake 90 years ago from a woman's perspective.

《马尔智蜜月日记》在浙江大学沈弘工作室及谢小珮女士翻译版本的基础上，由我和阮少茜反复修订校译，最终定稿。

After rounds of reviewing and editing, Ruan Shaoqian and I finalized the translated draft of March's Honeymoon Diary by Sarah Shay and Zhejiang University's Shen Hong Studio.

张　倩

Zhang Qian

2016 年 6 月

June 2016

目录

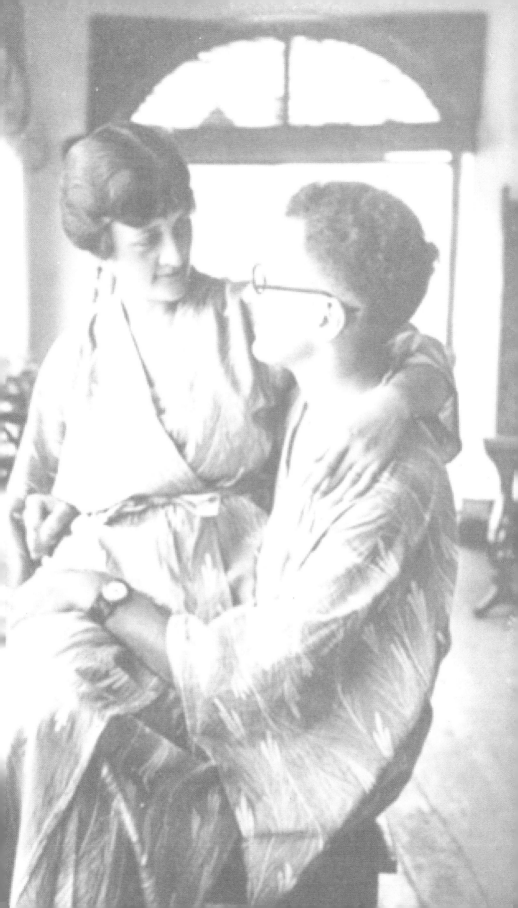

We arrived in Hangchou on time, and were met by a servant who took charge of our bags and brought us quickly to our destination. We had written about staying places and Dorothy had inquired of one Miss Rebecca Wilson. Miss Rebecca had then arranged for us to have an entire house, furnished, with a competent staff of servants and all the trimmings for the month for a very reasonable figure. The house is that of the foreign teachers in the Union Girls' School, located in a very pleasant compound only a short walk from West Lake, the most famous beauty spot in China, the place for which Hangchou is famous. Arrangements were made for the cook to provide food for us, so we have all the comforts of home with a minimum of inconvenience. Sleeping porches, and everything are here for our enjoyment. We had a good supper, played the victrola for a few records, and decided to retire to the sleeping porch.

　　我们按时抵达杭州，一个仆人前来替我们提取行李，并很快将我们带到了目的地。来杭州之前，我们曾写过几封信寻找住处，多萝西咨询了一位吕贝卡·威尔逊小姐。威尔逊小姐帮我们安排了一套价格合理、家具完备、有专职仆人的房子，还准备了其他蜜月所需的用品。这套房子是联盟女校（弘道女中）专门为在校的外国教师提供的，居住环境很不错，距离西湖仅几步之遥。西湖是中国最有名的景点，杭州也因此闻名遐迩。仆人中有专门的厨子，让我们有着家一般的舒适及便利。这里所有的一切我们都可以享用，包括凉台。用完美味的晚餐，打开手摇留声机听了几张唱片，我们决定去凉台。

道德学社杭州分社的大门
The gate of Hangchow branch of ethical institute

马尔智在弘道女中校园内
March in the Union Giris' School, Hangzhou, July 1925

Here was a perfectly good birthday, and good day
for a birthday. It was warm and we were not in the
mood for doing much chasing around, so we stayed in
the house until tea time, had tea and then went for
a walk. This was my first sight of West Lake, and
I was quite content. The east shore of the lake,
and part of the north, is occupied by hotels, summer
residences, and the like (the city is on the east
shore of the lake) and some of them are pretty bad.
Hills surround the lake on three sides, and the
city fills the plain on the fourth. Most of the
buildings sink into a common blend from a little
distance and one can quite forgive them, and, under
certain conditions even enjoy them. One, though, has
irked me from my first sight of it, and probably
will continue to bother. On the shoulder of a hill
north of the lake is a slender and graceful Needle-
point Pagoda. From city and lake it is a commanding
landmark, and we have good view of it and the hills
from our sleeping porch. Just at its foot, so near
as to almost crowd it off the hill, a foreigner, Dr.
Main, has built an ugly two-storied barn of a resi-
dence that looms up white and ghoul-like from almost every angle. It is difficult to see the slim
pagoda without that square white atrocity intruding
itself upon the scene. It is a barbarity of bar-
barities and it alone whould make loyal Chinese
weep and wish us all to depart for our own shores
or worse.

　　我们度过了一个完美的生日，今天也特别适合过生日。外面很热，也没心
情去做其他的事情，所以就呆在家里喝完下午茶。茶后出去散步，这是我第一次
看到西湖，感觉非常宜人。沿湖东岸（杭州城就在西湖东岸）和北岸的部分区域，
都被旅馆和避暑别墅占据着，有些建筑是非常糟糕的。西湖是三面环山一面城的
格局，从不远处望去，大部分的建筑都融为一体，这些都是可以接受的，甚至在
某种情形下还是可以欣赏它的。但是有一个建筑从看第一眼起便心生厌恶，而且
有可能会继续被困扰。沿湖北面的宝石山山脊有一座纤细而优雅的针形塔（保俶
塔），无论是从城市还是湖面上望过去，它都是一个有地标意义的制高点，站在我
们的凉台上，可一览（保俶）塔及（宝石）山的至美风光。塔下，有座外国医生梅
恩建造的、丑陋的二层谷仓式楼房，和保俶塔挨得如此之近，几乎盖过了塔的风
头。无论从哪个角度看，这座白色楼房就像个幽灵。要想在你的视野内摒弃这幢
白色方形建筑，只看见纤细的保俶塔，简直是不可能的。这行为真是野蛮中的野
蛮，只会让忠贞的中国人哭泣着诅咒我们滚回自己的地方，或甚至更严重。

保俶塔
Baoshu pagoda

We walked on over the causeway to the far end
of Imperial Island, and back again in time for supper. After supper we stood out on the porch as the
far hills flamed red and little tongues of sunset
flame lapped along their peaks. I had discovered
some music within my abilities and amused myself on
the piano for a time before moon was high.

我们沿着白堤一直走到御岛（孤山）的尽头，在晚餐时间及时返回。饭后，我们站在凉台上看远山一片火红，夕阳西下只露出一点红舌盘踞在峰顶。我尽我所能找出些音乐，自娱自乐地弹了会儿钢琴，直至月亮升起。

从窗洞里眺望西湖
Saw the West Lake through a
window opening

从桥洞里眺望西湖
Saw the West Lake through a
bridge arch

杭州金沙堤上的玉带桥
Jade Belt Bridge on Jinsha Bank of Hangchow

西湖边的民居
Folk houses on the side of the west Lake

Again it is a good day, thougha bit hot. To
avoid the heat we went out for a walk immediately
after lunch. Rather paradoxical that, but a fact
none the less. We wandered along the streets until
we reached our objective, Shu Lien Chi, most famous
fan shop in China. Hangchou fans are the fans of
the people who are, and Shu Lien Chi is the shop
that has made Hangchou famous in modern times. It
is curious to step into a large and busy Chinese
schop and see framed certiffcates of award from
world expositions on the walls. We looked over
some few samples of their stok for nearly an hour,
and came away with four. I got a large sandalwood
fan I had been wanting, and a small black wu-mu one
to wear with my dinner jacket; Dorothy a wide blue
one and tiny silver one. We explored our way back
to the lake through stone-paved narrow byways, and
finally reached the shore. We were warm, so hurried
home for tea, rested a while, and took our lunch
out in a boat on the lake in time for sunset.

　　尽管有些热，但今天仍不失为美好的一天。为了避暑，午饭后我们便出去散
步了。这听起来似乎有些矛盾，事实也是如此。我们沿街闲逛，直至目的地——
中国最有名的舒莲记扇庄。杭州的扇子一般以人命名，舒莲记扇庄让杭州在现代
也扬名天下。走进宽敞而忙碌的商店，看到墙上居然挂着装裱的、出自于世界博
览会的各种奖状，感觉很特别。我们花了近一个小时在他们库存的一些样品中挑
选，离开时买了四把扇子。一把是我一直想要的大檀香扇，一把是穿晚礼服时用
的小乌木扇。多萝西则是一把蓝色的大扇子和一把小巧的银色扇子。我们穿过石
板路的街巷，几经周折，终于回到岸边。我们感到燥热，急匆匆地赶回家喝茶，
休息了一会儿，带着餐食泛舟湖上，欣赏落日的余晖。

The boatman paddled us towards the Island of the Three Pools of the Moon's Reflection, and by the time we rounded the point the sunset glow had faded and the fifth month's full moon was climbing from cloud to cloud up the heaven. Still, so still the boat slipped out from under the willows into the light that we caught one of the little stone pagodas that rise in the lake marking the spots where the three deep pools that harbored spirits are, squarely in the golden path of the moon's reflection. Who would not come from half the world away to see the Three Pools of the Moon's Reflection catching and tossing from one to the other the gold of the fifth month's full round moon?

船夫带我们划向三潭印月。当我们绕过一个转角，落日的余晖已经散尽，仲夏夜的圆月穿过一朵朵云攀上天空。万籁俱寂，唯有小船静静地划过柳梢，划进月光，我们望见三潭的一座小石塔，挺立湖中，恰好就在那如金色小道般的月影之上。小石塔标记着三个深潭的位置，据说这里镇压着精灵（传说湖中有黑鱼精出没）。谁都会从世界的另一端，来一睹仲夏夜圆月在三潭中浮光若金、交相辉映的景象。

三潭印月
Island of Three Pools Mirroring the Moom

三潭印月的石塔
Stone Tower on Isiand of Three pools Mirroring the Moom

Many boats were on the lake and there was
much sweet music as we circled around toward the
Imperial Island. The Chinese know what music fits
a scene like this and the many various instruments
work together for beauty to them that love the lake
and the night and the moon.   If I had started
when I was a small boy as many Chinese small boys
start, I might now be able to play the long slim
bamboo flute that is made for a man to play when
he sits alone in the moonlight and whose sound is
so delicate that only a few can listen and hear it,
and so plaintive sweet beauty walks abroad on feet
that leave pink fragrant lotus in her train.

湖面上有很多船只，我们绕着圈划向御岛（孤山）时，感受到了周围美妙的音乐声。中国人知道美景配美乐，各种不同的乐器在一起演奏出他们所钟爱的夜、月、湖的美好。如果我像中国很多小孩那样从小就开始学习乐器，也许现在我就可以演奏一曲竹笛。竹笛很适合在月色下独处的人吹奏，其音色细腻悠远，只有极少数人能欣赏，或温婉或凄凉，令岸上的美人也步步莲花，缓缓而行。

The most noteworthy characteristic of the day
was the heat, of which there was plenty. We spent
most of the time in the house, out on our special
upstairs porch, but ventured out in the afternoon
to find a photographer to print some pictures for
us. Having found him we left our negatives and
found a bench by the side of the lake. We were sitting there talking of nothing in particular when
my old friend T. B. Chang happened along. We had a
joyful reunion as usual, to the amusement of the
bystanders who did not understand our affectionate
caresses. He had just arrived and had not known
that we were here, though he had received our announcement and was much excited about the wedding.
It was amusing to hear him tell how he had opened t.
the announcement and read the names "The Reverend
and Mrs. Harry Fleming Rowe" half a dozen times,
wondering who they were to be sending him things,
and then how he saw the name "Mrs Benjamin Franklin March, jr.", and had nearly fallen over in his
surprise. He was accompanied by his brother Thomas
and a friend Mr. Tung, a secretary in the Hangchou
Y. After a little general talk they left and we
came home.

今天最值得一提的就是"热"，一整天都如此。大部分时间，我们都呆在家中的长廊里，但下午还是冒着酷暑出了门，找一个摄影师替我们冲洗照片。我们留下底片便离开，在湖边找到一处长椅坐下闲聊时，正好碰上我们的老朋友张竹平先生。意外相逢，让我们像往常一样又搂又抱，旁人恐怕很难理解我们的亲昵行为吧。他刚到杭州，并不知道我们也在这里，虽说他也收到了我们的结婚请帖，并为此感到十分激动。我们饶有兴趣地听他讲打开请帖时，把"哈利·弗莱明·罗牧师及夫人"的名字念上六七遍，一直在猜是谁寄给他的，然后当他看到落款"本杰明·富兰克林·马尔智先生"时，诧异得几乎晕了过去。和他一起来的是他的弟弟托马斯及一位朋友，杭州青年会的秘书董先生。聊了一小会儿，他们便离开了，我们也起身回家。

With a very nice rain we have had a real break in the weather, and have had some heart to work a little. We set out early this afternoon to see some of the things on Imperial Island. It is said that Hangchou is noted for three things, for the West Lake, for the Bore, and for the Sixteen Lohans which were painted originally in the T'ang dynasty by one Kuan Hsiu. They were cut in stone to preserve them, and are now models for pictures of these saints. Thither we directed our way, stopping to see on the way the tomb of Hsu Hsi Lin, the leader of the first revolution, and the Memorial Hall of the Three Faithful Ones. Both are noteworthy for their simplicity, but we did not stop. We came to the park where the old Lohan pagoda is located, to find it occupied as a yamen. We were directed into a side courtyard that glooked like a very ordinary yard of a dwelling house. A couple women and a child or two followed us in, and we were joined by a soldier and another young fellow. We stepped into this hall, in the center of which is a stone pagoda, sixteen sided, with an inverted lotus of stone by way of a cap. The whole thing stood about fifteen feet high, and seems to be called pagoda because there is nothing else to call it. On each of the sixteen faces was one of the tablets

一场及时雨，总算让我们有了片刻的喘息，也有了一些工作的心情。下午，我们早早出发去孤山游览。据说杭州有三张金名片：西湖、钱江潮和最早由唐代贯休绘制的《十六罗汉图》。为更好地保存，罗汉像被刻在了石头上，如今已成为绘制佛祖的范本。我们是冲着十六罗汉像去的，沿途看到了徐锡麟墓及三烈士纪念亭。徐锡麟是清光复会的领袖。这两处都因风格简洁引起了我们的关注，但并未留步。我们来到古老的罗汉塔所在的公园，发现此处已用作衙门。经人指点，我们径直走向侧院，那里看起来很像一个普通的宅院。

each of the sixteen faces was one of the tablets
of the lohans.   Many of the ancient paintings have
been preserved in this way, and the most famous
writings of the ages are all on stones. The original
painting or writing is pasted on the stone, and then
the design cut through it. The cutting is usually
quite shallow, but enough to show up well, and to
make rubbings possible, by which means copies are
available for scholars and connoisseurs. At either
side of the pagoda of the lohan were tablets, one
with a picture of a saint on the front and a Kuan-
yin on the back, the other with writing. The room
was full of tables, beds, cabinets, baskets of vegetables and old silk cocoons. There was so much
junk piled around in back of the pagoda and the ligh
was so poor that it was impossible to examine all of
the tablets with care. One would need much time for
moving the residents' belongings, and a good flash-
light to make a careful inspection. The saint on
the stone at the side was partially obscured by a
cabinet and the Kuan-yin by a chair. The dwellers
who had followed us in were eager to sell us rubbings. I had long been wanting a lohan set, and as
the rubbings were the best means for studying the
carving too, we purchased a complete pack. They seem
ed to be good, and to have been made from the stone.
That of course is not necessarily true as you will

　　两个妇女及一两个小孩跟着我们走了进来，之后一个士兵和一个小伙子也跟了进来。我们走进大厅，大厅中央摆放着一座十六面的石塔，塔顶反扣着一朵石质莲花。塔高约 15 英尺，之所以称之为"塔"，是因为找不到更合适的名称。

　　石塔十六面的每一面，都是雕刻有罗汉石像的石碑。许多古老的绘画，就是以这种方式保存下来的，那些历朝历代最著名的书法作品也都刻在石碑上。人们把绘画或书法的原作贴在石头上，然后把图案刻在上面。通常刻痕都比较浅，但足够清晰显现了，也让制作拓片成为可能，拓片可以为学者及鉴赏家提供复制品。罗汉塔的两侧都立有石碑，其中一块正面是佛祖像，反面是观音像，另一块则刻有文字。屋内放满了桌子、床、柜子、装蔬菜和旧蚕茧的篮子。有太多的杂物堆放在石塔背面，加上昏暗的光线，根本无法仔细看清所有的石碑。除要花很长时间搬动那些居民的杂物外，还需要一个光源充足的手电筒，才能清楚地辨认石碑上的内容。一旁石碑上的佛祖像几乎被一个柜子给挡住了，另一面的观音也被椅子遮住了。

remember from my account of my visit to Ch'üfu last
year. The squalor of the court and the cluttered
condition of the hall were most depressing. What
conclusion to draw we could not decide. Were the
lohan a greater treasure in hearsay than in fact?
Where they appreciated by scholars outside of Hangchou more than by the residents? Did closeness to
them, familiarity, breed contempt in the minds of
those who profited from their guardianship and from
the sale of rubbings? Or, tragic thought, did this
apparent mistreatment argue democratic indifference
to old treasures and lack of interest on the part
of those who should have cared? Is this modern re-
publican China? The Chihese have a faculty for con-
centrating their interest on a thing irrespective of
its surroundings, and perhaps the hall's condition
did not jar them as it did us; amd anyway there were
rubbings. It left me in such a mood that even the high
rocks of the beautiful public park, the peak of
the island, where Ch'ien Lung's palace once stood,
failed to restore my feeling of peaceful satisfaction with the world around me, - a mood which the
numerous photographers' shops on old pavilions only
aggravated.

　　尾随而来的居民，迫切地向我们推销拓片。我早就想要一套罗汉像了，因为拓片是研究石刻的最好样板，我们买了一套。它们看起来不错，像是从石头上直接拓下来的。但也未必如此，如果你记得我对去年参观曲阜的描述就应该知道。肮脏的庭院和杂乱无章的大厅，让人很沮丧。罗汉像的巨大价值是否言过其实？那些外地的学者，是不是比本地的居民更心仪这些罗汉像？对此，我们很难得出结论。那些从看护和出售拓片中谋利的人们，会不会因太过熟悉而心生轻蔑。或者，悲观地看，这些显而易见的不当行为反映的是，大众对传统财富的漠视及相关部门的不闻不问？难道这就是现代的中华民国？中国人具备不顾周边环境而专注于某些他们感兴趣事物上的能力，也许让我们感到沮丧的大厅环境并未让他们感到不安；不管怎么说，有拓片为证。眼前所见，让我的心情低落，即便是面对美丽公园里高高的假山、爬上曾是乾隆皇帝行宫的山顶，都未能让我回复平和而满足的心境来面对周遭世界。而那些开设在古老亭子里的众多照相点，让我的心情更加糟糕。

Fortunately we went on to the beautiful grounds of the West Lake Seal society where a goldfish pond, a cared-for rockery, and properly protected and honored stones of old West Lake scenes and modern writings and pictures made me happy again. We climbed to the top of the hill, where there is a modern garden, with interesting statues of scholars of the society, a lotus pond, pavilions and a stone pagoda. We sat and drank tea and looked out over the lake, and enjoyed ourselves for quite a long time. There are numerous small tablets with pictures of well-known members of this leading literary society of Hangchou, and innumerable samples of the writing of the members and others. Here we saw what the old tradition can do today if it takes an interest and is fired by some ambition. Two interesting statues are set in pleasant surroundings as though their subjects were taking their ease in the garden. They are cut of the common gray stone of the neighborhood, and the faces and hands are done with full expression while the draperies are but roughed-out in a broadly suggestive manner. They were rather satisfactory for their type of thing. At the little shop near the entrance we looked at many rubbings and some modern books of pictures and characters. Had I brought more money I should have carried home more rubbings. In a way it was fortunate that I did not, for now I shall have to return and that I shall be glad to do.

好在我们又走进了一个典雅的院落——西泠印社。那儿有个金鱼池，一座悉心修葺的假山，刻有老西湖景点及现代书画作品的石碑，也得到了恰当的保存。这些又都让我们兴致勃勃。我们爬上山顶，那儿是个现代公园，有西泠印社著名学者的生动雕像、一汪荷花池、几个亭子及一座石塔。我们喝着茶欣赏西湖美景，享受了好一会。这里有很多小石碑，镌刻着西泠印社知名社员的画像及社内外许多人的书法作品。在这里我们可以看到，在兴趣及壮志雄心的激励下，古老的传统在今天依然能被传承。两尊生动的雕像，被安置在舒适的环境中，好似自己本人在花园里休憩一样。雕像所用石材，取自于周边常见的灰色岩石，脸部及手部表情生动，衣褶则采用了粗犷及写意的手法。在同类雕像中，这是令人相当满意的。在靠近出口的小店里，我们翻阅了一些拓片及图文并茂的现代书籍。如果身上带着更多钱的话，我肯定会抱更多拓片回家。但没多带钱未尝不是好事，为此我反而开心，因为不得不再来。

自西泠桥的北端眺望西泠印社
overlooked xiling Seal Society from north ned of xiling Bridge

西泠印社的摩崖题记
Carving inscription on one cliff in Xiling
Seal Society

自西泠桥的桥洞下眺望保俶塔
Looked Baoshu pagoda into the distance under a bridge arch of Xiling Bridge

In the afternoon, after another rainy day, we ventured out to the photographers to get our prints, which were very carelessly done so that we shall send our negatives to Peking hereafter, and then looked for T. B. Cheng's house on the way home. We failed to find it, but he came in to call soon after we arrived here, so all was well. We chatted about sundry things, but will have to have along session to exchange all of the opinions we want to air for each other.

又是一天的雨。下午，我们冒雨去取冲印好的相片，相片印得很粗糙，看来要把底片寄到北京去冲洗了。回来的路上，想找张竹平先生的房子，未果。我们到家后，他又自己送上门了，也不错。我们闲聊了会，但如果要相互畅谈尽兴，则需要有大段的时间。

The day was largely occupied, as several of
its predecessors have been, in writing and getting
off numerous and lengthy letters. When it is not
raining just now it is apt to be warm, so we do not
leave the house much in the early part and middle
of the day. In the afternoon, however, we decided
to go out to the Island of the Three Pools of the
Moon's Reflection, partly to get the boat ride and
partly to enable me to get some sketches of the little stone pagodas in the lake out there. We landed
at the island's back-door, and stepped out to the
lotus pond through a short avenue of bamboos. There
we were confronted by a rare and lovely sight. The
water was black as a forest pool, as polished jet,
or well-rubbed lacquer. Motionless out of this polished glassy surface lifted the velvety soft green
leaves of the lotus sparkling with drops of mercurial
water, and the buds and full-blown flowers inimitably
pink with the happy blush the Buddha's favor brings.
We crossed the stone flagged Bridge of Nine Windings,
past the Triangular Pavilion, the temple now used
for the sale of photographs), a pleasant monolith of
rough fantastic stone embraced by flowering trumpet-
creeper vines, and came to the Swastika Pavilion. This
is a summer house of galleries laid in the form of the
ancient symbol. The galleries are lined with seats,
though they are not very wide. The whole occupies a
square perhaps fifty feet on a side at the edge of
pond. The island is little more than pond with a
tree-lined edge around it, and is not much more than
a couple hundred yards across in either direction.

就像前几日一样，今天的大部分时间，也都用来书写和寄出好几封长信。刚刚雨歇，气温转高，所以中午之前我们都没出门。然后到了下午，我们还是决定去三潭印月，一是为泛舟，二也想为湖上的小石塔画几张速写。我们在小瀛洲的后门上岸，穿过竹林短径，走近一片荷花池。呈现在我们面前的，是一幅罕见而迷人的图画，池水黝黑如林中深潭，如精心抛光的墨玉，又如打磨到位的漆器。水平如镜的湖面上，亭亭玉立着的是天鹅绒般柔软的荷叶，闪烁着如水银般来回滚动的水珠。或含苞或绽放的荷花，犹如受到佛祖的青睐，透出无可比拟的、娇羞的粉红。我们穿过石板铺就的九曲桥，经过三角亭（开网亭）、先贤祠（现为出售照片的商店），被凌霄花藤蔓爬满的、奇异又好看的石头（九狮石），来到卍字亭。这是一座用于避暑、按照古老佛教符号建造的回廊式亭子，廊道上排列着座位，倒是不宽。亭子占地约 50 平尺，靠近荷花池的一侧。小岛只比池子稍大一点，四周绿荫环抱，横竖直径不过几百码。

三潭印月岛上的荷花池
Lotus pond on Island of Three Pools Mirroring the Moon

三潭印月岛上的九曲桥
Nine-Turning Zigzag Bridge on Island of Three Pools Mirroring the Moom

九曲桥上的亭子
Pavilion on Nine-Turning Zigzag
Bridge

Crossing another set of bridges over another ~~particularxther~~ arm of the lotus pond we came to the pavilion at the edge of the lake. In front of us were the three small stone pagodas marking the spots where the Poet Su placed similar monuments many years ago to suppress the unruly spirits lurking in the three deep pools there. We spent an hour or so sketching and observing, then realized with a start that we were going to be late for supper. We hurried back to our boat, but not so fast as to miss the beauty of the very artificial island with its ponds, bridges, rocks, bamboos and pavilions. The wind was against us, so I soon took a hand with an extra oar and we got home not too late to enjoy our meal.

穿过另一组桥，我们来到荷花池的另一侧，靠近湖边还有一座亭子，前方就是三个小石塔，这是很久以前诗人苏东坡曾置三塔镇妖的地方。我们花了一个小时左右写生，突然意识到已经快到晚餐时间了。我们匆匆往船上赶，一路上又欣赏了一遍这优美的的人工岛上的池子、小桥、假山、竹林和亭子。船逆风而行，我用另外一只桨帮忙一起划，到家后晚餐也不算太迟。

    This afternoon, after a day of rain, we set
out for a little hike, to see what we could see. We
turned to the north along the lake, and I was interested in finding the end of the city wall. The wall
had formerly inclosed the city but in recent years
the section adjoining the lake had been removed and
the city had gone down to the water. The broken
end should have been not far from the lake and we
went to see. Near the spot where it was marked on
one of our maps we found remnants of it, ruined
mounds from which all of the facing stone had been
removed. Behind a large building belonging to the
Tao Te Hsueh She we came to the end of the old ram-
part itself. It was overgrown with weeds, and in
the wet it was not too easy of ascent. Workmen were
busy at the end cutting it down and filling a low
place inside of it. On an open field nearby soldiers
indulged in drill and rather childish artillery
maneuvers. Along the outside of the wall was a narrow cultivated strip between the wall and the lake.
The facing of the wall, formerly of heavy stone
blocks, is completely gone from this section for the
space of a mile or more. It seems not to have been
either so high or so wide as the walls of Paoting
and Peking. We strolled along the narrow footpath
on the top, alternately watching the canal, an old
moat, and the houses and men and fields and Needle
Pagoda on the one side, and the little paddies and

又一个雨天的午后，我们出门远足，想随处看看。沿着西湖的北面，我饶有兴趣地发现了城墙的最末一段。城墙之前是绕着杭州城修建的，近年来，靠近西湖的城墙已经被拆除了，城市一直延伸到湖边。断墙应该离西湖不远，我们决定一探究竟。我们根据一张地图上标记的位置，发现了城墙的残垣。从荒废的土堆来看，城墙的外贴面砖都被搬走了。在属于道德学社的一幢建筑背后，我们找到了旧城墙遗址的末段。这里不仅杂草丛生，而且湿滑，很难攀爬上去。工人们正忙着开挖遗址部分，并把挖出来的土填到里面的一个洼地里。在附近的一块空地上，士兵们正专注于操练非常幼稚的炮兵动作。城墙的外侧，在湖与墙之间，有块狭长的庄稼地。约一英里长的城墙上，原本用于砌墙的沉重石块都已不知所踪。看起来这里的城墙，不如保定城和北京城的高大宽阔。我们在城墙上面狭窄的小路上溜达，左顾右盼，一边是运河、老护城河、屋舍、行人、田野和保俶塔，另一边则是一块块小稻田和房屋。

我们遇到了几个小孩，还有一头在人迹罕见的城墙上吃草的水牛。沿着城墙

houses on the other. We passed several small boys
and their buffalo, the latter grazing along the un-
frequented top of the wall. Following the wall and
its attendant canal we came to a corner where the
wall once stood foursquare around a court between
two gates. The wall is there, and the gate openings,
but the old doors and guard house have gone from the
inner gate and are but remnants at the outer. We
stopped to speculate, to admire and ancient pai-lou,
and to watch the people; then we turned back and retraced our steps along the way we had come. The wall
appeared to be no better beyond the gate then it had
been where we had walked, though along the railroad
side, the other side of the city, we had noticed it
in good repair, apparently, as we came in. Some of
these old walls might well be kept as monuments, but
it costs money to keep them, and where is that to
come from?

和运河，走到拐角处，原本是两道城门之间由城墙围合而成的四方庭院。城墙还
在，门洞大开，但内城门原来的门和护卫的门楼已荡然无存，外城门也只剩下一
些残迹。我们不时停下来，或思索或欣赏古老的牌楼，看来来往往的行人，然后
原路返回。城门之外的城墙，似乎并不比我们之前走过的那段更好。在进杭州城
时，曾在城市沿铁路线的那一侧，看到修缮得较好的城墙。部分老城墙是可以作
为古迹保存下来的，但保护需要的大笔资金又从何而来呢？

This afternoon, after another rainy day, we went into the city to look at shops. Though I had bought a couple fans for me only a week ago I wanted now to get another, a bamboo fan carved with bamboo leaves, something I had long been desirous of possessing, and I wanted to paint it with a picture of the Three Pools and to inscribe a verse on the other side, after the Chinese custom. We wandered along to the fan shop and bought the fan I wanted and a new one for Dorothy, and some papers. Then we poked some more and got me a stalwart, very masculine oiled paper umbrella, one of the kind for which Hangchou is famous, and another little thing I had long thought of getting when at last I should come to this city. So we wandered, stopping here and there to look at this and that. Hangchou is an interesting city. There are some excellent broad xx streets, well-paved with hard gravel-topped paving, and some fine looking modern shops, banks, and business buildings. Most of the streets in the new section opened by the removal of the wall are wide and well-paved. We live on such an one. But when one passes a few of the larger buildings and fine banks on his way along the main street, one plunges suddenly into a thoroughfare not twenty feet wide, stone-flagged, made into an arcade on a sunny day

今天又有雨，下午我们进城逛商店。虽然一周前，我已经给自己买了两把扇子，但我还想买一把心仪已久的扇骨上刻有竹叶的竹扇。按照中国的传统，我想在扇面上画一幅三潭印月图，并在背面题诗一首。我们一路闲逛到扇子店，买了把我想要的，也给多萝西买了一把，还买了些纸张。之后又逛了其他店，我买了把牢固的、适合男人用的油纸伞——它是杭州特产之一，也是我来到杭州一直就想买的另一样小物件。就这样，我们走走停停，逛逛看看。杭州是个有趣的城市，这里有宽阔气派的街道，铺着坚硬的砾石，有一些时尚的店铺、银行和商厦。大部分的街道，都是拆除城墙后开辟出来的，宽阔而平整。我们就住在这样一条街上。但是，当你沿着主街经过几幢大楼和气派的银行后，你会突然出现在一条不

stone-glagged, made into an arcade on a sunny day
by the awnings and advertising banners of the shops.
Here one finds the famous fan shop, paper shops, silk
shops, ink shops, and shops for the purveyance of
an infinite variety of necessary and desirable com-
modities. It is interesting to think that through
the changes that have come upon the city since his
day it may be possible that the streets are not
substantially altered in location and direction,
and that once he may have trod the very flags we
walk so carelessly.

足 20 英尺宽的街面上，路面铺着青石板，沿街店铺的晾棚和广告牌，挤挤挨挨地连成了可以遮阳的拱廊。

在这里，你可以找到有名的扇庄、纸铺、绸庄、墨店，以及其他各式店铺，可以买到各种必需品和称心如意的商品。街道所在的位置和走向，并未随着城市的变迁而发生实质性的变化。一想到我们漫不经心地走过的石板路，也许曾留下马可·波罗的足迹，就觉得很有趣。

杭州御街上的文锦坊
Wen Jin workshop on the imperial street of Hangzhou

杭州元升线帽洋货庄
Yuan sheng alien Yarn and cap products shop of Hangchow

Having determined that we would venture an
entire days diversion in a hike into the hills we
gave orders, encouraged by a bright sunset, for the
cook to make us next day a lunch to be carried in
our hands. This morning after breakfast we packed
the lunch, a few books and bits of paper and pens,
into the packsack, and set out for the north shore
of the lake. Circling around the temple of the big
Buddha we came to the place of ascent and climbed
the stone-paved pathway that led to the summit of
the hill. Though the path led up through shade-
giving trees we were hot and steaming before we
emerged gratefully into the cool breezes of the open
spaces. The pagoda itself, called, colloquially,
the Needle or Needle-Point Pagoda because of the
shape of the ruin, dates from the tenth century. It
stands on the crest of an arm of a hill to the north
of the lake, overlooking the lake and city, quite
the most prominent landmark. It is about a hundred
feet high and it crowned by a bronze shaft decorated
with sundry rings and points. The wooden parts have
all gone now, and most of the openings have been seal-
ed, but broken places here and there reveal the fact
that it was once possible to climb inside to the last
of the pagoda's seven stories. Brick patterns and

　　昨天日落时分的晚霞，促使我们决定今天到山中远足一整天，并吩咐厨师准
备好随身携带的午餐。一早用完早餐，我们把午饭、几本书、纸笔打包好，向西
湖的北岸出发。我们绕过大佛寺，拾阶而上，直至山顶。尽管一路绿树如荫，仍
闷热难耐，爬到开阔的区域后的那阵凉爽，叫人满心欢喜。这个建于公元 10 世纪
的（保俶）塔，因其残存的形制被称为针塔或针尖塔。它位于西湖北面山脊的高
处，俯瞰西湖和杭州城，是最显眼的地方。塔高约 100 英尺，青铜塔刹，装饰有
许多环和凸起的乳钉。木质部分已荡然无存，大部分的开口都已经被封死，随处
可见的裂缝显示：该塔曾经可以从塔内登上最高的第七层。
　　值得注意的是，砖砌样式、叠瓦装饰及陶土外框的那些窗户并非虚设，而是

tile trimmings and terra-cotta frames of what are now false but may once have been true windows, are noticeable. By the use of my sighting compass I ascertained that this pagoda and the now demolished Thunder Peak Pagoda once marked the north and south poles, as it were, of West Lake. Next to the pagoda is the white foreign house of Dr. Main, which we admitted, has an enviable location in spite of graceless appearance. We passed it quickly and went on along the narrow path to the summit of this hill, where huge rocks are piled like hand-placed pebbles on a mound. I scrambled around trying to get a picture of the pagoda without the house, and then we sat in the cool of a cave for a while before beginning our descent. From the top of this hill, where there is a stage with a stone balustrade, one has a superb view of the lake, the city, the Ch'ien T'ang river, the sea, and the surrounding countryside of Chekiang.

有实际用途的。我用观光指南针测了下方位，敢肯定该塔和已经毁圮的雷峰塔正好位于西湖的南、北两极。保俶塔旁边，就是梅恩医生的白色洋房。我们必须承认，那幢房子尽管外观突兀，却占据了令人羡慕的地理位置。我们迅速绕过这幢房子，沿着狭窄的通道登上最高处，这里巨石就像鹅卵石山般堆叠在一起。我攀缘其上，试图拍一张没有那座洋房的照片。下山之前，我们又在一个凉爽的洞口坐了会。山顶上还有个有石制栏杆的高台，此处远眺西湖、城市、钱塘江、大海及周围一带浙江乡野，风光无限。

自宝石山上眺望保俶塔
overlooked Baoshu pagoda on the top of Baoshi Hill

自阳台上眺望保俶塔
Overlooked Baoshu pagoda on balcony

雷峰塔
Lei Feng Pagoda

We were heading in a general westerly direction
and now, instead of returning to the road, we let
ourselves down the side of the hill to the west by
means of steep narrow paths through the brush, until
we came to the road ascending to the Taoist monastery
of Ko Ling. First there was a stone pavilion where
water seemed to spring from the rocky hill, then a
tree-bordered trail, and finally the outer courts of
the temple itself. This outer court seemed to have
been both cut out of the stone and builded up in a
kind of valley, and it was a remarkable example of
artificially natural assistance to nature. The rock
wall at the end of the garden, just under the main
temple gate, had been partially laced with the
fatastic rockery work familiar in Chinese gardens,
and from the pool at the bottom, to the wutung trees
in their niches, to the temple gate at the top, it
made a perfect picture. Within the temple comfortable chairs were set out and the two old priests
both over sixty, immediately set about preparing
twa for us. There is nothing of note about the plac
except a well said to be one of thirty-six dug by
Ko Hung about 320 A.D., the inventor of the dyeing
process. The whole place was repaired about five
years ago by a merchant who grew wealthy in the war,
and most of the bells and censers, of quaint old

下山时，我们并未原路返回，而是穿过灌木丛，沿着狭窄陡峭的小路一路往西，最后走到上葛岭抱朴道院的大路上。最先映入眼帘的是一座石亭，亭边泉水从岩石间汨汨而出。沿着林荫小道，最后来到抱朴道院的外院。外院位于山谷间，犹如从岩石上凿出来一般；这是一个虽由人作，宛若天成的杰出范例。院子的尽头，道院大门之下的石壁，正对着中国园林中常见的、怪石嶙峋的假山，从一池清泉，到掩映其间的梧桐树，再到高耸的大门，一幅多么完美的画面。道院给我们提供了舒适的椅子，两个年过六旬的老道士忙着为我们沏茶。道院内并无特别之处，除了一口井，据说是公元 320 年，由染色工艺发明者葛洪挖的三十六口井之一。五年前，一位因战争发了财的商人，出钱重修了这座道院。大部分的钟和

design, bear the date "ninth year of the Chinese
Republic." After resting a bit we went on to the
top of the hill, the highest point along the north
shore of the lake, where there is a pavilion and
monument marking the spot from which Ko Hung used
daily to greet the rising sun. After another good
look around the countryside we continued on our
westward way down toward the Cave of the Purple
Cloud.

香炉，都是按照古老的形制设计的，刻有"民国九年"的字样。我们稍作休息，
又继续往上爬，沿湖北面的顶峰上有座亭子和一块碑，据说葛洪每天在此恭候冉
冉升起的太阳（初阳台）。环顾四周的田园风光之后，我们继续下山西行，前往紫
云洞。

Up a bamboo shaded path we went to the gate of the little temple from entrance to the gate is gained. There we descended a flight of steps into the damp and cool interior of the fairly good-sized cave, a cave which has been made artificially with the clever semblance of naturalness that is apparent in so much of the Chinese landscape work, a naturalness which has its best qualities in its artificiality. Probably because of the difference in temperature and humidity between the cave and the outer world, the cavern was full of a thin purple mist which justifies if it does not give the name of the place. We proceeded through a passage and a small room and another ascending passage to the shrine cave where, carved out of the rock were images, elaborately painted and gilded, of the Buddhist trinity. We sat for quite a while in the cool dampness watching the images in the sunlight that came down from the opening at the side near the roof of the cave, and then went back as we had come to the stage overlooking the first hall. There were tables and benches in front of a shrine to Kuan-yin, and we ate our lunch and drank tea.

Inscription on doors and door posts and by the side of the images. 佛陀彌阿無南

顺着蜿蜒而上的竹林小径，我们来到一个小寺院门口，这里便是（紫云）洞的入口。直下台阶，进入潮湿阴凉的洞内，里面空间很大。紫云洞巧妙利用了自然地形，因地制宜，就像中国园林呈现出的最高境界——人与自然的和谐。也许是因为洞内外温度和湿度的不同，洞内氤氲着一层紫色的薄雾，紫云洞因此而得名吧。我们穿过过道及小石屋往上，走到神龛前，经过精心彩绘及描金的西方三圣像，是直接从岩壁上凿出来的。我们在阴暗潮湿的洞内坐了好一会儿，端详着光影里的佛像，光线是从洞顶一侧的露天处洒下来的。之后我们回到可以俯瞰第一进大殿的平台，那儿的观音像前，摆着一些桌子和长凳，在此我们用了午餐并喝了茶。

注：门上、门楣上、佛像边都写有"南无阿弥陀佛"的字样。

We went down through shrines and graves to
the lake, and turned to the right along the motor
road until we came to the stone-paved road that
leads off through the the graveyards to the Gem
Spring of the Dancing Fish. A curious burial custom is observed here in places. Long low houses are
built resembling small garages, with eight, ten or
more doors. Within there are cells where coffins are
placed in what seems to be a rather temporary form
of permanent burial. The country through which our
path, carefully trimmed though traveled only by
pedestrians and chair bearers, ran, appeared to be
neglected, for the graves were often quite overgrown with the luxuriant weeds and brush that are
common in this part of China. Soon we found our
way through trees and graves and rice paddies to
the Ch'ing Lien Ssu, the temple of the Gem Spring.
The temple is noteworthy for its gilded images,
and for an inner hall where there are two walls
filled with glass-doored cases containing eighty-
four images of lesser deities. These images here
are about three feet in height, and well preserved
and brightly gilded. There is little aritistic meri·
in any of the images here, though.

我们经过佛龛和墓地，下山到了湖边，向右沿马路西行至石子路上，经过坟场，就到了"玉泉鱼跃"。这里有个奇怪的丧葬习俗：一长排的矮房子开了八扇、十扇或者更多的门，就像一个个小车库似的。虽说是永久墓室，但小屋内的棺材却像是临时摆放的。我们沿路经过的那些乡村，虽说修整得很整齐，但由于只有一些行人和轿夫经过，显得尤为荒凉。墓地里长满了灌木和杂草，在中国的这个地区很常见。经过树林、墓地和稻田，很快我们找到了清涟寺，又称玉泉寺。值得一提的是该寺的镀金佛像，内殿两侧墙壁的玻璃柜上，陈列了八十四尊小佛像，高约 3 英尺，明亮镀金，保存完好。然而这些佛像的艺术价值并不高。

玉泉鱼跃
Fish Jumping in the Jade Spring

玉泉附近停放棺材的排屋
Row house near the Jade Spring that were used for placing coffins

The main feature of the temple is the spring
of the dancing fish in a court at the side. Here is
a pool about the size of an ordinary swimming pool
in a Y at home full of water that appears to be
the color of light green jade. It cannot be very
deep, though the bottom is not distinctly visible.
In the center of the pool is a small stone pagoda,
and at the east end a little open garden plot and
pavilion. Around three sides of the pool are galleries like porches of the temple rooms behind them
Close to the railings are set tables and chairs
overlooking the pool. Within the pool are hundreds
of carp, a fish of note in China, ranging in size
from a few inches to several feet in length, and
color from black to bright red-gold. When one sits
at a table cakes, like flapjacks made of flour and
water, are brought, and it is amusing to break these
and throw them to the fish, who veritably dance in
their efforts to get them. Little sweet cakes and
dried fruits and tea are served to the people who
serve the other cakes to the fish, and one can stay
here indefinitely feeding the fish, watching the
people, and drinking tea in the cool comfort of the
gallery by the pool. As we sat watching the fish
this thought occurred to me:

Carp in the Gem Spring dance for bisquits,
Men in offices dance for gold;
I'll be a fish in the jade-green water free;
Time enough to be a man when I'm old.

清涟寺的主要景观，是庭院一侧的玉泉鱼跃。池子大小如同美国 Y 型家庭的游泳池，池水呈浅绿的翡翠色。虽然池底并非清晰可见，但估计池水也不会太深。池中央有尊小石塔，东面是开放的小园圃和亭子，沿池的三面回廊像是后面寺庙的门廊，靠近栏杆处，摆了些桌椅，便于观池赏鱼。池内游弋着数百条中国特有的品种——鲤鱼，颜色或黑或金黄，长度从几英寸到几英尺不等。当你坐在桌边，把带来的小糕点掰碎扔到池子中时，鱼儿会争先恐后地跳跃抢食，甚是有趣。小甜点、干果和茶，是提供给客人享用的，但人们愿意一直坐在那里，投食喂鱼。在池边回廊阴凉处喝着茶，看着这些人，观赏着鱼儿，不禁浮想联翩：

玉泉鱼跃为觅食，
职场人拼图钱财。
唯愿长作池中鱼，
待到年衰复为人。

We left presently, and made our way back along the
pleasant grass-grown stone-paved avenue through the
trees and graves. Coming once more to the lake side
we stopped at the magnificent tomb and monument of
Yao Fei. Most noteworthy here is the architecture
and decoration of the newly completed buildings. The
main hall is in accordance with the regular principle
of Chinese building, but the interior is brighter
and cleaner than most such places and this is largely due to the unusual use of clear glass windows in
the clerestory. The walls are white, with four
large characters cut and paitned in them, and a
number of honorific verses are inscribed on tablets
hanging from walls and pillars. The shrine is gold
and red with an image of the gentleman. The gardens
are attractive and the grave not unusual. The roof
of the main hall is adorned with four groups of
warriors near the four corners which vary the traditional roof design of Chinese buildings in a not
unpleasant manner. This is a very good example of
what can be done in modern building along traditional
lines. I hope the work is stoutly and honestly done.
One cannot always tell what is behind the red paint.

盡
忠
報
國

　　不久，我们就离开了，沿着芳草萋萋的石子路往回走，穿过树林和墓地，再次来到湖边，在宏伟的岳飞庙（墓）和纪念牌坊前驻足。这里最引人注目的，是新落成的建筑以及装饰。主殿格局遵循中国建筑的普遍法则，殿内使用了玻璃天窗，比同类建筑明亮干净得多。白色墙壁上刻写了"盡忠報國"四个大字，墙上、柱子上悬挂着褒扬的对联。红色镀金的神龛里，供奉着英雄岳飞的塑像。坟冢并无特别之处，倒是庭院挺吸引人的。主殿屋顶的四只角，装饰了四组勇士，虽与中国传统建筑的屋顶极为不同，但也并非不妥。以何种方式让现代建筑遵循传统样式，这无疑是个很好的案例。我希望该建筑结实牢固，并无半点马虎。至于红漆底下是什么材料，无人知晓。

岳王庙的正殿
Main Hall of Yuewang Shrine

岳飞神龛
Yuefei Shrine in Main Hall of Yuewang Shrine

We went on along the lake shore and home to
our baths, passing on the way the New Hotel, a
monstrosity in European style, very good of its
hybrid kind, and numperous gorgeous small temples.

　　我们沿着湖岸回家沐浴，途经新新饭店。那是一个欧洲风格的奇怪建筑，中西风格混搭得还不错。此外还路过几个极好的小寺庙。

We stayed at home and read and painted fans
these four days, for it rained most of tne time,
and I was a trifle indisposed. There has been
little curtailment of my regular activities, but
I have stayed pretty well in one placedoing a minimum of moving around. This afternoon, however we
are going out to explore the world again, and to
see if we can find me a haircut.

过去的四天，大部分时间都在下雨，我们只能呆在家里看看书、画画扇面，略感不爽。尽管稍微减少了些日常活动，但在同一个地方呆着也不错。不过今天下午，我们准备再度出门探寻，并找家理发店。

Venturing out this afternoon we want first in search of a barber shop, and having found a fairly clean and very elaborately tiled and white-painted one which Dorothy had spotted previously I gave myself up to be trimmed. The young fellow cut my hair with great care and nice precision, then asked what else I wanted and I told him a shave. So shave he did. Having finished the space normally allotted to the razor, gleaning until not a bit of recognizable stubble was left, he started off in the manner of Chinese barbers making smooth the surfaces of their Chinese customers. First it was all around my ears, then the ears themselves. Inside and out he went, back and front. Then he got back onto my face and wandered up around my forehead. Leaving my eyebrows and lashes he scraped diligently all around my eyes, then carefully whittled off my nose. I was very much amused at the performance, for often I had watched it happening to someone else but never before had I subjected myself to such treatment, and I was the more surprised since this particular barber shop proclaimed themselves as barbers in the foreign manner. I had made up my mind that I would stop him when he got the little knives and started up into my nose and down into my ears, but he did not venture and I was spared. He put some tonic (I think it was really only a strong odor) on my head and dismissed. "How much?" I asked. "Two dimes and seven coppers," he replied. He changed a dollar for me and I gave him the extra loose coppers, about a dozen, by way of a tip. The whole business had cost me less than twenty-five cents in our money. Just now there are about thirteen silver dimes to a dollar, and a two dime piece is just almost nothing at all. Such a cleaning for such a price I never had before.

下午出门，先找理发店。我们进了一家白墙青瓦、相当干净的店，这是多萝西之前看中的。小伙子以极大的耐心，仔细为我修剪头发，然后问我是不是需要其他服务，我告诉他想要刮刮脸。剃刀刮过的地方，一丁点胡茬子都不留下。接着他开始了让中国客人面容光洁的中国式手法：剃刀先是耳朵周围，接着耳朵上，里里外外，前前后后滑动，然后又是脸部、前额来回游走。除眉毛和眼睫毛外，他又努力地刮过眼睛周围的每一个毛孔，然后小心地修刮我的鼻子。如此刮脸方式甚是好玩。我常看别人理发，但从没想过自己也会受此礼遇。让我更为讶异的是，店员居然说他们用的是西式手艺。我已打定主意，如果他把剃刀深入我的鼻孔或耳朵眼，我就要阻止他了，所幸的是他并未这么做，我也就释然了。他在我头发上抹了些发油（我觉得那只是具有某种强烈气味的东西），理发结束。"多少钱？"我问道，"两角七个铜板"，他回答。我给了他一元找零，并给他十几个铜板作小费。整套服务只花了不到 0.25 美元，现在一美元大约可以兑换 13 银角，两角钱几乎微不足道。如此干净，如此价格，从未遇到。

It rained while I was being made beautiful,
and Dorothy was out looking around. When she came back
she had a small package containing a blue silk Hangchou wedding belt of the old style, made like a tubular
fishnet, with long, long fringe. At home once more I
put it on and we admired me greatly.

理发时，雨还在下。多萝西就在附近逛逛。回来时拎着一个小包，里面装着一条杭州婚礼用的老式蓝绸腰带，像带有长长流苏的管状渔网。回到家我把它系上，好好欣赏了一番。

This afternoon we set out for the Imperial Island, stopping on the way at the Monastery of Manifest Congratulations. We crossed a stone bridge over a pond walled with red walls on three sides, to the main entrance. The right half was in use by soldiers, but a priest at the other entrance assured us we could go in. The entrance contained the usual four gods, though of unusually large size, and the laughing Amida Buddha. The main hall was a great barn-like structure, red on the outside, and a dull undecorated red on the inside. A wide portico sheltered huge dragon and phoenix lanterns. Within the hall was the great Buddha, the iron image, which alone did not perish in the fires of T'aip'ing days. Lohans lined the walls, and images of the Thousand-Handed Kuan-Yin and of the mother Kuan-Yin stood at the rear. The second hall was more interesting, containing the old altar of the oath, one of two cr three in China. This was a stone stage about thirty feet square and four feet high, surrounded on the top by a stone balustrade carved in a cloud pattern. Each side of the stage was divided into five panels, fairly deeply built, and in

下午，我们去了趟孤山，途中在昭庆寺稍作停留。寺院前有个水池，三面都围着红墙，穿过水池上的石桥，便是主入口。寺院的整个右半边，都被军队占用了，在另一个入口的僧人示意我们可以进。进门处照例是四尊佛像（象征风调雨顺），体型异常高大，还有一尊笑口常开的阿弥陀佛。正殿空间很大，谷仓式结构。外墙红色，内部暗红色，并无装饰。宽大的柱廊上，挂着龙凤大灯笼。殿内唯一未在太平天国火灾中烧毁的，是一尊铁质大佛像。墙边立着罗汉，佛像身后是千手观音和送子观音。第二进大殿则更为有趣，中间有一座古老的受戒坛，是中国仅存的两三座之一。受戒坛是一个 30 英尺见方、4 英尺高的石台，顶部的围栏刻有云纹。石台的每一侧，都分成五组图案深嵌其间。每一组图案，都有高约两英尺的三尊彩绘泥塑神像。据我了解，它们似乎是阴曹地府中的判官和小鬼。

昭庆寺的大门
The qate of Zhaoqing Buddhist Temple

昭庆寺内的石碑"古然灯佛降生之地"
"Birthplace of Dipankara Buddha" of stele in
Zhaoqing Buddhist Temple

昭庆寺大殿内的戒台
Jie Tai in grand hall of Zhaoqing
Buddhist Temple

自昭庆寺的东侧眺望保俶塔
Overlooked Baoshu pagoda from east side of Zhaoqing Buddhist Temple

each panel were three brightly colored mud gods about two feet high. They resembled the judges and other lesser demons usually associated with Buddhist hells more than anything else I know. On the stage was a plain white plasted screen in front of which sat a gilt Buddha, the Pi-lu-fo, or Buddha who has entered into Nirvana. He was not distinguished, though said to be the only one in Hangchou. The building, as barnlike as the first, was very lofty and pigeons made their homes among the rafters and in the great lantern. Since the military occupation the building has not been used for the old ceremonies of the administration of the oath and the burnings of the head.

石台上有一面素净的白石膏屏风，前面端坐着一个镀金佛像——毗卢佛，或是某位已涅槃的佛。这尊佛像虽说是杭州仅存的一尊，但也无特别之处。和正殿一样，该殿也是谷仓式结构，屋顶很高，鸽子在椽子上和大灯笼中筑起了巢。自从军队占据后，寺院就再也没能举行过传统的僧众受戒和剃度仪式。

A new wing along the side held quarters for
monks, and a dining hall was set with many places. It
is said that there are usually from fifty to eighty
monks here, practically all transients. They told us
that they did the work of building the new wings themselves, and they do all of the upkeep and cleaning.
It is notable that here the temples are as a rule in
better condition of upkeep and cleanliness than in
the north, and there is more appearance of active
participation in worship. In many of the monastery
temples there are benches or cushions for the priests,
sometimes to the number of several tens. In the
north the buildings are mostly of older appearance,
ornately decorated, and decadent. Here the buildings
seem for the most part to be fairly new, and to have
been put up because there was felt a need for them,
so that they are more utilitarian. Most of the inter-
iors are finished in plain wood, painted red, or unpainted, and the columns and beams without their
lacquer and plaster coatings often look very thin. It
is plain that they were put up when there was not
too much money available, probably shortly after the
Taiping rebellion, when many of the temples and
halls here were destroyed. I am also observing that
what seemed to be remarkable in the exposing of
gods in glass cases in the temple at Yu Ch'uan, is
a very common thing in temples and monasteries here,
where walls of main temple halls are apt to be filled in this way in much the same manner as the walls
of a library are filled with books.

大殿一侧新的厢房，是僧侣们的宿舍和饭堂，饭堂设置了很多位子。据悉这里一般会住 50 到 80 位僧人，通常都是临时挂单的。他们告诉我们说，这些厢房都是自己建的，所有的维护和打扫也是由他们自己来。值得注意的是，这里寺院的卫生和维护都比北方做得好，从外观看起来，人们敬拜活动也更活跃。这里很多寺院庙宇，为信众们提供的长凳或蒲团有时多达几十个。北方的寺院建筑，大多外观陈旧，装饰繁复却又颓败不堪。这里的大部分建筑，看起来都很新，被建起来是因为有需求，所以它们也更实用些。室内多采用木构，或上了漆，或者就是裸露的，那些没有上漆或抹上石灰底的柱子或梁看起来很细。显而易见的是，太平天国起义后，许多寺庙佛堂都被毁坏，这些建筑重建时的资金是捉襟见肘的。我还观察到：就像在玉泉寺里看到的那样，将佛像陈列在玻璃柜里的做法，在这里的寺庙是相当普遍的。主殿墙上的佛像，也都以同样的方式陈列，就像图书馆里放满了图书的柜子那样。

We walked along the island road, and I had a
desire to see the Chekiang Public Library. We were
permitted to go in, and go in we did. This place
has a very decent building in a rather painful rur-
al-country-seat-modified-bourgeois-chateau style of
architecture. The building was built for this pur-
pose. In the main hall is a good light well under
a sky-light, and a "grand staircase"leading to the
second story. The building was started just before
the end of the Manchu dynasty. In this central
hall is the English catalog. They have about eight
thousand English and foreign books, many of which
are in a city branch. As I glanced through the
cards it seemed that most of the books were of the
textbook class, including many textbooks of the
English language. I introduced myself as the lib-
rarian of the School of Chinese Studies, and a very
pleasant young fellows took us upstairs and showed
us the carefully locked rooms containing the collection of the libraries of K'ang Hsi and Ch'ien
Lung. The books are all bound between wooden covers,
and kept in cases made of fragrant wood, finished
black on the outside with the name of the collection
and the number of the case in gilt characters. Some
of the books are kept in modern cases, open, with
screen doors. Chinese books need to be aired and

我们沿着孤山路走，很想去看看浙江公共图书馆。经允许，我们得以进入。
在纷纷将乡村屋舍改造成庸俗的别墅式建筑风格的地方，有这样一幢非常得体的
建筑，它当初建造时就是为了这个目的。大厅采用天窗采光，非常亮堂，一个宽
大的楼梯通向二楼。这幢建筑是满清王朝覆没之前开始建造的。中央大厅有英文
目录，这里大约有 8000 册英文和其他外文书籍，有些藏在市区的分馆。我大致
看了看卡片，大部分都是外文教材，包括很多英语教材。我介绍自己是汉学研究
学院的图书馆员，一位和善的年轻人引我们上楼，参观那些上了锁并珍藏有康熙、
乾隆朝图书的房间。所有书的封面和封底都是木质的，并保存在香樟木匣子里，
外面则是黑底烫金的书籍名称和编号。有些书保存在现代的书柜中，推拉式的门
敞开着，中国图书需要定期透气日晒。

sunned periodically. We looked at some of the
printed and written books in both collections, at
an old Sung dynasty book said to have been printed
from iron plates, and at an old Buddhist sutra inscribed in very fine engraving on palm leaves, in
what is probably Pali or some Indian script. When
we came away our guide presented me with the two
volumes of the complete catalog of the two impor-
tant old collections.

　　我们看了些收藏的刻本和抄本，有本古老的宋代刻本，据说是铁制雕版印刷。还有一本古老的佛经，非常精细地刻在棕榈叶上，可能是巴利文或是印度的梵文。当我们要离开时，这位向导赠送给我两本康、乾两朝旧藏的完整书目。

At the West Lake Seal Society we spent a couple
hours looking at rubbings and reproductions of
famous paintings by contemporaries. When we came
away our collection of rubbings had been somewhat
augmented. We took a boat home across the lake.

我们在西湖边的西泠印社呆了几个小时，观摩了拓片和名画的当代复制品。
离开时，我们搜集的拓片数量又有所增加。随后坐船回家。

We set out fairly early this morning with our lunch, and hired for the day the boat we had used once before to go to the Island of the Three Pools. We set out to follow the lake shore, heading south and west. We stopped at several temples along the way, as we came to them. The Ch'ien Wang Tz'u is being restored by the Chao family, and they are doing a very good job of it. The buildings are in excellent condition, tablets are carefully housed, and, most interesting, workmen were busy making new shrines, modelling mud gods and putting gold-leaf on carved doors. This will be a gorgeous place when finished. Another little temple had little to recommend it as a temple, but its courts and lotus pond made us want to stay there for many days. The outer court was green with four towering phoenix trees, and six plantains, and bamboos against white walls, and lotus through moon doorways all make pictures. The Thunder Peak pagoda is but a mass of bricks now, and there is little left to tell its former grandeur. The Monastery of Pure Compassion has a beautiful forecourt with a red screen bearing the words

今天我们一早就带着午餐，雇了之前曾经用过的那条船，出发去三潭印月岛。船沿着湖岸，向西南方向前行。一路上，经过寺庙，我们便会停下来看看。赵氏家族正在修复钱王祠，这是一项很有意义的事情。整个建筑保存条件良好，许多石碑都细心地安置在室内。最有趣的是，工人们都忙于做新的神龛，制作泥塑神像的模型，并把金叶敷设在雕花门上。竣工后，这里会变得金碧辉煌。另一个小寺庙，从寺庙的角度来看并不太值得推荐，但它的庭院和荷花池，倒让我们很想在此逗留几天。外院种着四株高大的凤凰树，六株芭蕉树，满眼绿色，翠竹掩映着白墙，透过月洞门的莲花，风景美如画。雷峰塔，只剩一堆残砖破瓦，昔日的宏伟气势荡然无存。净慈寺的前院很美，隔着小莲池，红色照壁上写着字。

facing the temple from across a lotus pond. Before
the temple gate is a wide terrace, and within the
courts are spacious. The halls pile up onto the
hillside, with galleries connecting various chapels
and dwelling quarters. The monks tell us that this
is a T'ien T'ai temple. Several of the halls are of
bare wood without paint or decoration, and are quite
attractive to me. The miraculous well is rather amus
ing. Through this wood was transported by Buddha is
response to prayer asking for assistance in rebuild-
ing the temple. A priest lowers a candle into the
well until it rests on womething which he claims is
end of a log of wood sticking up. It might be, but-
He is scarcely courteous is one goes off without
leaving a tip. It is noteworthy, though, that there
is practically none of trailing visitors around in
these places, and the relief from paying admissions
and tipping begging dogging soldiers and priests is
great. We ate lunch in a side lagoon, waited under a
stone bridge while a beating rain passed. Took refuge in the bare open pavilion of the Dragon King
on the Heart of the Lake Island, and came home.

院门前宽大的台阶，里面的院落很宽敞。大殿依山势而上，一进连着一进，曲折的回廊，连接着各个殿堂和寮房。有僧侣告诉我们，这是天台宗的寺庙。有几座大殿的木结构未经油漆或装饰吸引了我，而那口神奇的井更是不可思议。传说这口井是佛陀应了祈祷者的要求，用来运送木材，以协助重建寺庙。一位僧人将蜡烛降落到井下，直至无法再降落，他说这就是一根圆木的末端。事情也许就是这样的，但是佛陀并未顾及礼节，未留下任何暗示就走了。值得注意的是，这些地方几乎没有游客尾随，不用买门票，也没有士兵和僧人跟在后边乞讨小费，感觉不错。我们在池塘边吃了午餐，暴雨袭来时，我们在石拱桥下避雨，又在湖心岛的龙王亭（即湖心亭）躲了会雨，而后回家。

杭州湖心亭
Mid-lake pavilion of Hangzhou

Most days we manage to occupy well with one
thing and another, reading, writing, enjoying each
other's company, but today, though pleasantly was
rather uselessly occupied. In the afternoon we strolled into the city to see what we could see. We got
us some candy, bought some more fans, this time for
gifts, saw a famous ham shop, and a medicine shop
which rambled through many old courts like a veri-
table labyrinth, where there were many cages of
deer whosehorns are scraped to make some very val-
uable and highly prized remedies. We took time to
note various things of interest on the street. There
are many shops where they manke the large wooden
gongs that are used in public and private Buddhist
worship. Most of these are carved out of large or
small solid blocks of wood, and the best of camphor
wood. The streets are remarkably plesant to smell i
the vicinity of such shops. Then there are the
shops where they make the Hangchou lacquer. Hangchou lacquer is not as good as the Fuchou lacquer,
but it is intersting to pass a shop and see con-
fection boxes outside with the first coating of

大多数的日子我们都安排得很充实，事情一桩接着一桩，读书写作，享受相
互陪伴的快乐。但是，今天虽然也很愉快，却只是徒劳地耗去了时间。下午，我
们进城溜达，想到处看看。我们买了些糖果，又买了些扇子用来送人，看了一家
火腿店。穿过许多迷宫般的老院落，来到一家药店，这里有很多养着鹿的笼子，
鹿角被用来制作成价格昂贵的药材。我们花时间观察街上各种有趣的事物。许多
商店都在制作公共或私人礼佛仪式上使用的大木鱼，大多是从大小不一的整块木
头上凿出来的，最好的是樟木。这些商店附近的街道上，可以闻到宜人的木头香
味。还有些商店，是做杭州漆器的，但不如福州的漆器好。有趣的是，经过一家

what looks like gray mud drying on them. There
are embroidery shops where onemay stop and watch
the making of gorgeous coats and curtains and other
draperies in tne process of ornamentation. The deft
ness of the men and boys who do the work is rare
to behold, the manipulation of the spools of gold
thread as they move them here and there along the
pattern catching down the thread with silk of some
other hue to give the proper tone to the piece.
Hangchou is also noted for its scissors, and the
schissor shops are prominent, with rows upon rows
of bright and shining tools displayed in cases
along their walls. It is good to walk in the city.

店铺，放在外面的糖果盒第一涂层，像是刷了灰色泥浆，并在晾干。有一些刺绣
店，人们可以驻足欣赏华丽的外套、窗帘和其他布幔纹饰的制作过程。这些男人
和男孩们的娴熟技艺是难得一见的，他们熟练地操作着金线轴，按照图样来回移
动，金线之下交织着其他的丝线，构成了一幅配色恰到好处的刺绣。杭州也因剪
刀而出名，剪刀店内沿墙陈列着一排排装在盒子里的明晃晃的用具，尤为显眼。
在城里闲逛，显然是极好的。

It pleased our fancies today to try a ride
through the country by horseback. We had asked
the boy to see about horses, but at supper time
the report was that there was no chance to hire
any. However, this I was wakened by the clatter of
hoofs on the sidewalk, and looking over the porch
railing I saw horses below. The boy came tearing
upstairs to tell us the cost for the day, and we
arranged a bargain. We dressed and ate our breakfast
and in due time I was astride of a white mare and
Dorothy of a bay gelding, and the ma-fu followed on
a little bay. We followed the paths along the lake
to what is known as the Long Bridge. In one place we
passed a section where the city wall has been torn
down, and where the debris of bricks and small stone
is being used to make a new boulevard, which will,
in all probability, eventually encircle the lake.
We went around back of Thunder Peak, through the
court of the Monastery of Pure Compassion, and out
among the rice fields into the hills. Out among the
hills and paddies here it reminds me much more of
Japan than of anything else I have seen in China.
Many of the hills are adorned with graves, most of
which are overgrown with underbrush and trees until
one would not know them save for the protection the
sanctity gives to the vegetation. Some of these
graves are exceedingly elaborate, high mounds, with
stone stages, terraces, flights of steps, tablets,
arches and the like. Along the valley to Tiger

今天我们兴致大发，试着骑马出去郊游。我们曾让小伙计去找马匹，但昨晚
饭时，他回复说无马可租。然后一早，我就被路旁哒哒的马蹄声惊醒了，倚着凉
台栏杆往下看到了马儿。小伙计飞奔上楼告诉我们一天的租金，我们讨价还价了
一番。穿好衣服，吃完早餐，立刻出发。我骑着一匹白色母马，多萝西则骑着红
棕色阉马，马夫骑棕色小马跟随。我们沿湖策马前往长桥，途经一堵毁损的城墙，
残砖及小碎石，已被用来铺筑一条新的大路。这条路终将可能绕湖一周。我们绕
过雷峰塔，穿过净慈寺的院子，又在稻田间穿行进了山。如此景象，倒让我想起
了日本，甚于所有在中国所见。这里的许多山头，可见坟墓，其中大多数已经被
丛生的灌木及杂树湮没，谁会想到它们便是使其神圣不可侵犯的保护者。其中也
有一些坟墓很讲究，有高耸的土堆，石砌的台子、平地、阶梯、墓碑和拱门等等。

马尔智夫妇骑马去虎跑游玩
Benjamin March and his wife were riding towards Tiger Spring for a tour

虎跑的钟楼
Bell tower of Tiger Spring

虎跑内的二门
The Second gate of Tiger Spring

Run one grave particularly impressed me. It had once been a very imposing one with a semi-circular walled pool in front, two high stone columns reflected in the pool, a fine approach, and then the grave itself with its tablets, just at the foot of the hill. Now there is a tangle of small trees and brush. The two pillars stand pathetically reminiscent among the green things, and vines clamber over the broken stone coping of the pool. The moisture helps the growth of abundant vegetation over the hills, and the innumerable graves preserve it, though the population is not so dense as to constitute a serious menace to every blade of grass as happens in places in the north.

沿着山谷去往虎跑寺的路上，有座坟墓令我印象深刻。它一度非常气派，前面有一个半圆形石砌的池子，两根高大的石柱倒映在池中，一条较好的便道通往墓和墓碑。现如今，两根石柱被小树及灌木缠绕着，悲悯地矗立在绿荫间，仿佛在追忆往事。藤蔓在池边的碎石间蔓延。这里的湿度，有利于山上茂盛的植被生长，不计其数的坟墓也保护了植被。不过，这里的人口并不密集，不会对植被造成威胁。这要是在北方，就不会如此了。

We came to the Monastery of Buddha's Image, where the main image is said to be modelled over the mummy of a priest who died here a thousand years ago. The authenticity of this is difficult to prove, for the image looks like any other of its kinds, though tablets attest the genuineness of the figure. This monastery is a rambling old place, and in one hall we drank tea, and from another stepped out to a little pavilion on the hillside at the foot of a giant old tree that must date at least from the T'ang dynasty. I guessed T'ang and the little old priest told me I was right, that the tree was more than a thousand years old. The hillside was covered here with young bamboos, and there were some criptomerias. I was not able to ascertain just what kind of a tree the very old one was.

我们来到法相寺，据说这里供奉的佛像，是一千多年前去世的高僧的真身塑成的。这种说法难辨真伪，虽然碑文记录了该说法的真实性，但塑像看起来，与其他同类的塑像别无二致。这个寺院年久而杂乱，我们在一间厅堂里喝茶，从另一间厅堂走出去的山坡上有一座小亭子，山脚下有棵巨大的古树，至少可以追溯到唐代了。我猜想是唐代，一个瘦小的老和尚告诉我猜对了，这棵树已有一千多年了。山坡上种满了新竹，还有一些青松。我无法确定那棵古树的树种。

From here we partly retraced our steps, and then headed up into the hills again towards the Stone House Cave. Here again we found a temple, where a priest sat at a table pulling the rope of the log of wood that acted as a bell striker. The whole main hall had an air of newness that was not to our liking for it was a rather makeshift sort of newness. There is a little garden, and just behind this hall the entrance to the cave. This rather small room, carved out of the hillside contains a large gilt Buddha, and a number of lohans. The report is that there were originally 500 carved out of the rock and that now there are more nearly 1000. We examined some of these little figures, most of them not a foot high, seated on rock ledges and in niches all over the walls and ceiling of the cave. Some of them had stone bodies, and a few had badly bruised stone heads. but most had modelled clay heads and many clay bodies. A few were gilded, but most of them were painted over with the red varnish that is used in preparation for the application of gold leaf, but looking as though they never expected the leaf to be applied. Up on the hillside were two more minor caves. The garden was nice and we sat under an open portico to drink tea and look at the trees and rocks and cave.

从这里我们又折回了一段路，然后继续走进山林，前往石屋洞。在这里，我们又发现一座寺庙，一位僧侣坐在桌旁担任敲钟手，牵动绳木撞钟。整个主殿是那种我们并不喜欢的簇新，因为它是一个相当新的临时性建筑。大殿后面有个小花园，再往里就是石屋洞的入口了。石屋洞是个相当小的空间，是从山崖间凿出来的，供奉着一尊巨大的镀金佛像和一些罗汉。据说最初这里，在岩石间刻了五百罗汉，现在已有近千尊了。我们观察了一些小佛像，大多数不足 1 英尺高，端坐在岩脊和壁龛里，遍布岩壁和山洞顶部。有些是石制的，除有些身体或遭严重损毁的头部是石制的，大多数都是泥塑，极少数是描金的。绝大多数被涂上了红漆，通常是准备再敷贴金叶的，但看来他们似乎并未打算再贴上金叶。往上走的山坡上，还有两个更小一点的洞。这个园子很干净，我们坐在廊檐下喝茶，看看树、岩石和洞穴。

多萝西坐在石屋洞的茶室里
Dorothy was sitting in a teahouse of Stone House Cave

石屋洞的洞口
Opening of Stone House Cave

The next visit was to the Cave of the Morning
Mist and Sunset Glow. It necessitated some rather
higher climbing, and the horses went slowly up the
stone paved pathway. Everywhere one wants to go here
there seem to be stone paved roadways wide enough
for horses or chairs. We passed through a small
village at the foot of the South High Peak, and
came to the dismounting place near a very modern
little house where a Chinese movie company was busy
at work on location. It was amusing to watch them
for a while, and consider the circumstances under
which a girl would stand out on an open porch and al-
low a man to paint her face for her. The company had
come in chairs, and the bearers improved their time
sitting in the gateway gambling. We walked up
the winding path to the cave. As we went up we
could see off towards the river the blue hills,
and on the hillside we passed through bits of
rockery and groves of trees of very satisfying
beauty. The cave faces due south, and opens onto
a small tree-lined terrace. The mouth has been
made imposing by a brick and stone arch. Within
the entrance are some fine tablets, and inside
are rock-cut figures of the lohans, Kuan Yin, and
several saints and Buddhas. These figures are really cut out of the rock, are nearly life-size, and

　　下一个参观点是烟霞洞。山势有些陡峭，马儿缓缓地走在石头路上。这些马匹或滑竿能到达的地方，都是人们想四处走走的地方。我们途径南高峰脚下的一个小村庄，下马处靠近一幢非常现代化的小房子，那儿一家中国电影公司正忙于外景拍摄。我们饶有兴趣地看了一会，揣测当时情形，一个女孩站在走廊上，让一个男人为她画肖像。电影公司的人是坐着滑竿上来的，轿夫们坐在门前赌博，打发时间。我们沿着弯弯曲曲的小路前往烟霞洞。我们一路远眺青山河流，并在山坡上经过一些假山与树木，错落有致，如此美景，令人心满意足。烟霞洞面对南方，通往一个绿草如茵的小平台。洞口是砖石结构的宏伟拱门。入口处有些精致的石刻，洞内的罗汉、观音、高僧和佛像，都是从岩石上直接凿出来的，真人大小，相当精美。

烟霞洞的洞口
Opening of Cave of Morning Mist
and Sunset Glow

在烟霞洞供奉的一尊石像
An oblation stone figure in the Cave of
Morning Mist and Sunset Glow

are fairly good. The cave is artificial and winds
back into the rock to no very definite conclusion.
An old man leads one back, carrying a candle, for
which service a remuneration of several coppers is
in order. Just at the side of the main Buddha
image is a large water jar, and in the bottom of
this numerous coins, probably of offerings. Be-
lieveing that Buddha would not mind we fished out
a silver double-dime that gleamed in the water,
and used it to pay the old man and the lady from
whom we bought a cake at the entrance.

　　烟霞洞是人工开凿的，迂回于岩石间，深不见底。一位老者举着蜡烛做向导，
服务酬劳需要好几个铜板。主尊的一侧有个大水缸，底下有许多硬币，大概是供
奉的钱。相信佛祖不会怪罪：我们从水底捞出一个隐约闪现的两角银币，用以支
付老人的酬劳，并在入口处的老妪那里买了块糕饼。

When we got down again we had a bit of an argument with our ma-fu as to whether we would go our way or his, and finally ended by going his way. This took us down a valley of rice paddies to the bright orange gate of the Tiger Run Monastery. Turning in at this gate, one of the most attractive I have ever seen, we followed up a long road lined with criptomerias and other trees, and follwed for a space by a little brook, until we came to the house at the main entrance to the monastery. There, nestled down among great trees, was this house, and beyond it a small pool and a bridge. As we looked up from the bridge we saw above us more trees, and the bright orange wall of the temple with a curved-roofed tower, and friendly gate, and many gray roofs. Other pavilions and halls circle around on the hillside, and workmen were busy bauilding a new gate to one set of build- where a shrine had just been brightly repaired. All of the buildings looked down on three pools of various levels, and all around were the hills and the forest.

下山时，我们因为是按照我们的路线还是他的路线走，与马夫起了点争执，最终我们还是顺从了马夫的路线。沿着这条路往下走，经过一条种水稻的山谷，直至虎跑寺橙色大门，这是我见过的最吸人眼球的大门。拐进大门，我们沿着一条长长的甬道走，两旁种着松树和其他树，再顺着小溪旁的空地，一直走到寺院的正门。庙宇坐落在参天大树之间，不远处是一个小水池和一座桥。站在桥上望去，我们之上是茂密的树木，橙色的院墙外飞出微翘的塔檐，火焰色的大门，鳞次栉比的青灰色屋顶。还有一些其他的亭子院落环绕在半山腰，工人们在忙着为一组建筑修建新门，里面有一个刚修好的色彩明亮的佛龛。所有的建筑，都俯视着落差不同的三潭水，四周是绵绵群山和树林。

Inside of the monastery we found halls and passageways and courts and goldfish ponds, and no one bothered as we poked around. Here again, as in several other places we remarked the glass cases of gods, and here we found one case only partly full. Inside were four freshly gilt lotus blossoms waiting for gods, and outside were half a dozen Buddhas, painted red ready for gilding, evidently destined for places on the flower pedestals. Some had paper steamers pasted on them ,and I judge they are both votive offerings and tokens of munificent contribution to temple maintenance. doubtless insuring perpetual supplication to the donors. Behind the central group in the main hall we saw again the group that we had seen more completely and more newly done and painted at Fa Hsiang Ssu, that of Kuan Yin standing on t he dragon head emerging from the water into which the carp's tail is disappearing before the Dragon Gate. The carp turning into a dragon as it jumps through the Dragon Gate is a well-known symbol of the scholar taking his degree. She is a t-tended by the Dragon King, and several other deities, including the God of War and General We T'o.

在寺中，我们于大堂、过道、庭院及金鱼池间闲逛，并没有受到打扰。在这里，又看到了装佛像的玻璃柜，如同我们曾提及的在其他地方的一样。我们还发现有个柜子只装了一部分：里面四朵新镀金的盛开着的莲花，静候佛祖降临。外面有五六尊佛像已上了红色的底漆，准备镀金，显然这些是要放到莲花座上的。有些佛像上贴着彩带，我判断这些是信众用于供奉及为寺庙维修作慷慨捐助的标注，无疑是为确保施主们的永久祈愿。在主殿中央群像后，我们又看到了曾经在法相寺看到的那组佛像，只是法相寺的佛像是新做的、更完整并且上了漆。那组佛像中的观音，脚踏浮于水面的龙头，鲤尾隐匿于龙门前。鲤鱼跳过龙门则成龙，是文人取得功名的象征。伴随观音左右的，有龙王等诸神，包括战神和韦陀大将。

We sat down in one of the halls to eat our
lunch and an old lady pointed us out to an open
pavilion at the foot of a rocky cliff, near the
well which is famous all over China as the source
of the perfect water for steeping tea. We ate our
lunch with the refreshing accompaniment of tea grown
in the valley and steeped in the water from the well.
After a little rest we went down to our horses, re-
gretfully leaving this beautiful place, and turned
down along the valley toward the Ch'ien T'ang River.

我们坐在一个厅堂用午餐，一个老妇指着岩壁下的一个敞轩告诉我们说，这
附近的井，就是闻名全国的适合沏茶的最好水源的源头。我们一边用餐，一边喝
着用此井水沏出的此山茶。稍作休息后，我们骑马下山，依依不舍地离开了这个
美妙的地方，沿着山谷向钱塘江前行。

On the bank of the river we came to the Six Harmony Pagoda. This is an old structure of masonry, dating from about 950 A. D. It is ~~xxxxxxxxxxx~~ 200 feet high, and as solid as when it was first made. The outside is all of wood, painted red, and is thriteen stories. The inside of masonry contained seven true stories. Openings through the tower adjust-the variation of height of the stories. The outer part is hexagonal, but the inner is octagonal, at least in the inside passages. The tower, in spite of its height, appears to be rather squatty, for it is of great diameter, 48 feet along each side at the base. The first five stories have gods in the center, as in the diagram, but the upper two are built around the pole that points the peak. From the top one

A. God
B. masonry, windows omitted

has a surpassing panorama of the hills and the river that winds away like a broad highway toward the far blue hills. As we stood there a little breeze came up and the junks along the shore quickly hoisted their sails and put out. Below us on the shore were the exceptionally ugly buildings of the Hangchou Christian College, with the one good looking structure, the chapel, tucked away back among the trees so as to be but little visible. Toward the city was the dirt of the sheds and little

我们来到江边的六和塔。这是一个古老的砖石塔，始建于公元 950 年，高 200 英尺，目前仍坚实如初。塔身外部均为木质结构，涂红漆，共十三层。砖石塔内部实为七层。通过外部的开窗来调整塔层高度的差异。塔的外部是六角形，但内部则是八角形的，至少从内部通道来看是这样的。塔虽然很高，但看起来有点矬，因为直径很大，塔基每一边均有 48 英尺。五层以下的中央，都供奉着佛像（如图），但顶上两层沿塔柱建造直至塔尖。站在塔顶，可以一览群山大川，钱塘江像一条宽阔的公路蜿蜒伸向远处的青山。在我们驻足之际，一阵微风袭来，沿岸的舢板迅速扯起风帆，扬帆而下。在我们下面的江岸上，有几座属于杭州基督教学院（之江大学）的格外丑陋的建筑，还有一座外观好看的教堂，掩映在树丛中，隐隐露出一小点。

杭州六和塔
Six Harmonies Pagoda of Hangzhou

眺望六和塔
Look Six Harmonies Pagoda into the distance

自六和塔上眺望钱塘江
Overlooded Qiantang Jiang River on Six Harmonies Ppagoda

多萝西坐在六和塔的窗台上
Dorothy was sitting on the windowsill
of Six Harmonies Pagoda

yards xxxxxxxx where wooden junks and steel tugs
were being built; the end of the railroad, and the
squalid houses and little shops. On a broad piece
of level river bank a squad of women repaired brown
junk sails.

往城区方向望去，有很多脏乱的棚户和小院，那儿有人在建造木舢板和铁制拖船；铁路的末端，有些肮脏的房子和小商店。在一段广阔平坦的江岸上，一小队妇女在修补褐色的船帆。

We started back up the valley down which
we had come turning toward the West Lake and Hangchou. It was already four o'clock and getting dark.
While we were in the valley it began to rain, and
to rain as if it would never stop. It grew darker,
and we decided to go straight home instead of on
to the Dragon Well valley as we had planned. Along
the rice paddies, up through ferns and brush over
hills, down through groves of bamboo, past mourn-
ful graves, and finally out to the edge of the
lake we made our way. We were comfortably wet
through, and still enjoying the ride as we came
at last to the big road, and knew that we were almost home. The ride had been a pleasant one, though
the horses were hard of gait and slow of pace. We
had covered much ground, and we had had a most
pleasant time in the hills and valleys and temples,
and we had seen many things. Altogether it was a
good day and we were quite happy when we got home.

我们开始回头沿着山谷往下，朝着西湖和杭州城走。此时已是 4 点，天色渐渐变暗。我们还在山谷里时，便开始下雨了，看样子雨是不会停了。天色已越来越暗，我们决定直接回家，而不是像之前计划的那样去龙井山谷。沿着稻田，穿过山间的蕨类和灌木丛上行，然后往下穿过竹林，走过阴森凄凉的坟墓，最后终于回到西湖边。尽管全身湿透了，我们还是觉得挺舒服，依然享受地骑着马直至走到大路上，我们知道马上就要到家了。这是一次快乐的骑行经历，虽然马匹的步伐坚硬而缓慢。我们走了不少路，在群山、山谷和寺庙中度过了一段最愉快的时光，也看到了不少东西。总之，今天是美好的一天，我们回到家时，都感到很愉悦。

Awaiting us here was a fine pile of mail
from America, both letters and magazines; and
after we had changed our clothes and bathed we
had a grand orgy of reading. Nothing could bring
a better conclusion to a fine day in the saddle
among beautiful surroundings than a hot bath, a
good supper, and a fine pile of home mail. Truly
this has been a good day.

在家中等待我们的，是一堆来自美国的邮件，有信和杂志。沐浴更衣后，我
们开始了阅读盛宴。在美景中的马鞍上度过一天之后，洗个热水澡，享用一顿丰
盛的晚餐，饱读一堆家书来结束美好的一天，是再好不过了。今天真的是美好的
一天。

Following what has become our custom we spent the morning at the house. Our upstairs porch is cool in the morning, andrather hot with the sun on it in the afternoon. I made an expedition into town to get some paper for these Memoirs, and then we had tea and went out for a boat ride. We crossed to the island of the Three Pools of the Moon's Reflection, and there were able to make some rather nice pictures. We circled the island and returned to our house. In the evening I developed a couple strips of film. One was quite successful, but the other not so good.

按照惯例，整个上午我们都呆在家里。楼上的凉台，上午都是凉爽的，下午在太阳的直射下相当炎热。我进城为这些日记买了些纸，然后我们喝完茶后便出去坐船，直抵三潭印月岛，到那儿是想拍些很棒的照片。我们绕岛转了一圈便回家了。晚上，我冲洗了两个胶卷。有一张相当成功，其他则都不太好。

三潭印月的九曲桥
Nine-Turning Zigzag Bridge on Tsland of Three Pools Mirroring the Moom

We set out right after lunch and took our
boat across the lake and up a little inlet to Mao
Chia P'u. There we started to hike along one of
the familiar stone-flagged paths through the rice
paddies and up toward the hills. After going up
for some few minutes we came at a small square
pavilion over a pool, bearing the label, Lung Ching,
Dragon Well. There we started up a series of
broad shallow stone steps, and these we climbed,
winding up past a wooded inclosure, until we came
to a kind of divide. We had passed an attractive
gateway of orange plaster and black wood wickets,
and to this we returned. Descending the path among
the forest trees we came to the temple, in rather
ill repair, but be fixed up, and went through it to
the beautiful spring on its northern side. This
spring comes up into a pool about six feet across,
from which the water descends by several artfully
made channels until it goes off down the valley. It
is a beautiful spot, with a path winding on up throug
to forest to the hilltop, and with stone benches, and
a small pavilion for the present refrehsment of those
who will stop here and drink of the tea for which the
valley is famous. We chose to drink, and sat by

午饭后，我们便划船跨湖经过一个小水湾到达茅家埠。在那儿我们开始徒步，沿着熟悉的石板路，穿过稻田，往山上走。走了几分钟后，我们来到池边的一个小方亭，匾额上书"龙井"。从那儿开始，我们顺着一段开阔平缓的台阶蜿蜒而上，绕过一段木质围栏，直至到达一个分界点。我们经过一道很吸引人的橙色石膏板大门和几道黑色的木质小门，然后又折回。沿林间小路往下，来到一座因破败而在维修的寺庙——是该修修了。穿过寺庙，就到了北面清澈的山泉。清泉注入约 6 英尺宽的池潭，向下流经几段巧作的水渠，直至流进山谷一泻而下。这是一处美景，一条小路蜿蜒而上穿过树林，便能到达山顶。这里有石凳，有个可在此歇脚和品茗的小亭子，这处山林因此而有名。我们选择在此喝茶，坐在潭边等

龙井
Dragon well

the pool while the cups of tea were brought out to
us. We loafed there, playing a bit in the icy water,
drinking the tea, talking to one of the two priests,
a man who had come from a famous monastery in Sze-
chuan, and making some photographs. We came away and
went down the hill through the forest of the temple
grounds, following the newly paved pathway. Near the
lower gate was a new little shrine, with three
images. Two of these were still unpainted, and we
would see that they had been made of camphor wood.
The carving was of rather sketchy character, but
not bad, and the fragarance of the wood must have
insured them life for many years.

着为我们上茶。我们悠闲地呆在那儿，拨弄着清凉的泉水，喝着茶，和两位僧人
中的其中一位聊天，他来自四川一座著名寺院，也拍了些照片。随后启程下山，
穿过寺庙中的树林，顺着新铺的小路往下走。靠近下面山门附近，有个新的小神
殿，内有三尊佛像。其中两尊还未上漆，可看出佛像是用樟木制作的，人物雕得
相当粗略，但还不至于太糟糕。樟木的香味，会让这些佛像保存很多年。

On the upper slopes of the hills and in patches throughout the valley are the tea bushes from which comes this famous Lung Ching tea. As a matter of fact not only the tea from the valley, but that from this entire neighborhood, is styled Lung Ching, and it is one of the best green teas in China.

We walked back to our boat, and returned to our house under a gorgeous sunset, in time to wash before supper.

在山地较高的斜坡处和整个山谷，种着一片片茶树，著名的龙井茶便产自这里。事实上，龙井茶不仅仅产自这片山谷，附近这一带所产的都是龙井茶，它是中国最好的绿茶之一。

我们回到船上，伴着壮美的落日回到家，沐浴，用餐。

In the afternoon we explored in the city.
We walked along trying one shop after another to
get some of the little wooden gongs the Buddhists
use in their worship. We wanted them made of camphor wood, but most of the small ones are of other
stuff. Finally we found them and went on our way.
We turned into one narrow little street by the
side of the canal and found it lined on both sides
with silver and jewel shops. They had tempting ar-
rays of jade and other stones. When we came to
the place where we must recross the canal we found
a little temple with a brught orange wall. The name
was the Shui Teh Ssu, or Water Virtue Temple. We
went in and found a single young priest busy with
his vespers. He sat in a chair that had a mosquito
net canopy over it, where, evidently, he spent most
of his time, reading or studying before the little
image of We T'o. On the main altar was a case containing twenty-four small images of various deities.
We should have enjoyed staying here and watching, or
talking to the friendly old Taoist priest that followed us in. But when we turned in a crowd of idly
curious people tagged us and began flowing into the
temple around us and behind us, so that we quickly
left. There were unusually many of them and they
were unusually brazen, and I do not like it. But, then,
we are aliens, and as a rule get better treatment
her e than most aliens do at home.

下午，我们在城里游览。我们沿着街走，试着一家接一家地逛，想买几个佛教徒在礼佛时用的小木鱼。我们想要樟木做的，但大多数的小木鱼都是其他材料做的。最后我们找到了想要的并继续往前。我们拐进运河边的一条小巷，两边金银珠宝店林立，店内陈列着诱人的翡翠及其他宝石。在必须重新跨过运河的地方，我们发现了一个橙色院墙的小庙，名为"水德寺"。我们走进去，发现只有一个年轻的僧人在忙于他的晚课。他坐在一把罩了蚊帐的椅子上。很显然，他在那儿度过了大部分时间，在一尊小的韦陀像前，或阅读或修行。主供桌上摆放着一个内有二十四尊各式小佛像的柜子。我们本应呆在这里好好观摩，或者和跟随我们进来的和善的老道士交谈。但在我们走进寺庙时，一群游手好闲又充满好奇心的人也跟着进来，并把我们团团围住，我们只能迅速离开。这样的人还相当多，而且脸皮很厚，我不喜欢这样。但是话说回来，作为外国人，我们在这儿受到的待遇可比在国内好。

杭州城内的另一条小水渠
Another small Channel in Hangzhou

杭州护城河

This morning we started for one of the most beautiful and satisfying spots it has been my fortune to see in China. We took the boat across the river, and instead of debarking at the regular landing we went up a narrow creek until we could go no further, then followed a path through the brush until we came out on the motor road. Along this we went, stopping at the foreign cemetery, where we paid our respects to the memories of Madame Stuart and her husband, Leighton's mother and father, until we came to the little cluster of houses, restaurants and shops around the imposing gate way to Lin Ying, the Retreat of the Spirits. Inside of the gate we seemd to be in a rare wooded park rather than in a temple. Ahead of us, up the road, was the Pavilion of the Sound of the Runnings Waters of Spring, on the Curving Dragon Bridge over the little stream that caroled to us over its rocks as it ran past in the narrow ravine on our right. To the left were the cliffs of the Mountain That Flew Over, and plainly to be seen were the mouths of the caves and some of the stone sculptures, among which are the oldest monuments in Hangchou. We wandered through the caves, not minding the Buddhas and Lohans. In one place a straight shaft of brightest sunlight struck upon the rocks at the bottom of a cave and bounced back upon the Buddhas lighting them as if by a fire.

今天一早我们动身去了中国最赏心悦目的景点之一。能欣赏那样的景致，也是我的幸运。我们坐船过河，并未在规定地点上岸，而是循着一条狭窄的溪流而上，直到船无法前行。然后沿着小路穿过灌木丛，直至走到机动车道。沿着这条道继续前行，在一座外国人的墓地驻足、默哀，这里长眠着司徒雷登的双亲——司徒夫人和她丈夫。之后，我们到达仙灵所隐之地——灵隐寺。这里有一小片房屋，有商店、餐馆，云集在寺院庄严的入口周边。进入山门，好似置身于一个罕见的森林公园中，而不是在寺庙里。顺着这条路，映在眼前的是春淙亭，回龙桥横跨小溪，溪水欢快地拍打着岩石，流过我们右手边的溪涧。左手边是飞来峰的峭壁，清晰可见一个个山洞的洞口和一些石刻造像，其中包括一些杭州最古老的遗迹。我们在山洞间徜徉，并不专注于这些佛祖和罗汉。有一处山洞洞顶正好能射进一束阳光，强烈的阳光直射洞底并反射到佛像上，犹如火一般将他们照亮。

灵隐寺的冷泉亭
Cold Spring Pavilion in Lingyin Temple

西面看灵隐寺回龙桥和春淙亭
Saw Hui Long Bridge and
Chun Cong Pavilion in
Lingyin Temple fron west

东面看灵隐寺回龙桥和春淙亭
Saw Hui Long Bridge and Chun
Cong Pavilion in Lingyin
Temple fron east

灵隐寺山门外的情景
Scene outside the gato of Lingyin temple

灵隐寺山门上所书"灵隐古刹"匾额
"Ancient Lingyin Temple" on a horizontal
inscribed board hanged over the gate of
Lingyin Temple

灵隐寺的理公塔
Li Gong Pagoda in Lingyin Temple

We cross ed the stream through the Pavilion
and wandered along the road in front of the Yun
Lin or Cloudy Forest Monastery watching the
water running over its partly natural and partly
paved course, and inspecting the sculptures that
stood out from the vines and general greenery on
the cliff opposite us. Near the temple gate were
two more pavilions and a large pool, a place that
looked quite good enough to swim in. All along
the way and all about us in this valley retreat
were fine large trees of many varieties, including criptomerias, pines, gingkoes, elms, wutungs,
and sundry others, with the lighter green of the
bamboo making white patches on the hillside and
feathery filling in spaces between other trees.

我们越过溪流，穿过春淙亭，在云林禅寺前的小路漫步，一边观察着水流过半自然半人工的河道，一边审视着对面峭壁上从藤蔓和绿叶间凸显的造像。寺前有两座亭子和一个大池塘，这个池塘看起来相当不错，都可以在里面游泳了。沿途山谷，郁郁葱葱，树木高大挺拔，有柳杉、松树、银杏、榆树、梧桐等。山坡上，斑斑点点的翠竹，犹如一片片轻柔的羽毛，穿插在万树丛中。

The first hall of the temple was dim and
high. The four great kings stood guard in the
shadows and the laughing Buddha greeted people in
a friendly manner as they came in the door. The
woodwork was generally in dull red, but the beams
and rafters were all decorated in designs in red,
blue and green on a white ground. This use of the
white ground gave a very strange appearance to the
decoration. When we came out behind the Buddha, by
the image of We T'o, we sat down on the doorsill to
contemplate the scene before us.

　　寺中第一进大殿高而昏暗，四大金刚守护在暗处，弥勒佛则在入口处笑迎天
下客。殿内木作几乎都是暗红色的，而雕梁画栋处都是在白底上用红、蓝、绿三
色描绘的。使用白色底子，让整个装饰看起来很怪异。弥勒佛像后面就是韦陀像。
我们坐在门槛上，沉思着眼前景象。

Through a large tree-filled court, terraced up and grass-grown, ran the straight wide avenue to the ste s leading up to the main hall. This great building was three tall stories in height, bright red and yellow in the sunlight. It stood majestically above the broad stone galleries approaching it, and towered above the giant trees themselves. On each side of the inclosure were minor shrines.

穿过一个大树环绕、绿草如茵的大庭院，中间一条笔直宽阔的大道直通主殿前的台阶。这座雄伟的建筑有三层，每一层都很高，在阳光的照射下，其红色和黄色显得更加亮丽。它巍然高耸在宽阔的石廊和参天大树之上，两旁则分立着小佛龛。

We approached the main entrance of the shrine and bowed in awe before the three great gold images of the Buddhist trinity. In one corner was a desk where incense and candles were sold, and worship here by the laity was continuous. Before the altar table were candleabra so high that step ladders were used to trim and light the lights, and here were hassocks of what looked like palm fibre for the kneeling of many priests. Dull red robes with white lines in patterns like fresh laid bricks were carefully folded and waiting for their wearers. At an elevated desk to one side a single monk, with his red robe over his shoulder, sat reading from the scriptures.

走进大殿，我们怀着敬畏的心情，在佛教三尊金身前鞠躬。殿内一角有张桌子，出售香火和蜡烛给络绎不绝前来供奉的信徒们。供桌前的烛台很高，要爬上梯子才能修剪和点燃蜡烛。地上摆着看似是用棕榈编成的蒲团，供僧侣们跪拜。折叠齐整的暗红色袈裟，上用白丝线绣着红砖一样的图案，正静候着它们的主人。一位身穿红色袈裟的和尚，独自坐在一侧高高的桌子边诵经。

Around in back of this group was a wall which took our breath when we first saw it. Fully fifty feet tall and thirty feet across was a mountainous background, peopled with deities of all kinds, before which stood Kuan Yin, the goddess of the dea. Here again she stood on the head of a kind of fish, and here again were the dragon king and the gate, but there there was no direct allusion to the Dragon Gate, and indeed the gate wore a quite different inscription. Two large gilt images attended the central one, and the eighteen Lohans walked on the waves, on fishes and frogs. It was a stupendous piece of religious symbolism, all in excellent condition and bright and clean.

The panels in the altar tables were small carvings, gilt on the highlights and with the faces of the people painted like ivory. They were carefully and skillfully done, and wisely covered with glass.

在这群佛像后面是堵墙，当我们看到它的第一眼便深吸了口气，足有 50 英尺高，30 英尺宽，以各路神仙齐聚群山为背景，前面立着南海观音。此处观音依然站在某种鱼的头上，也有龙王和龙门，但并没有直接注明这是龙门，而且门上的铭文更是大相径庭。两尊大的鎏金像相伴一旁，十八罗汉或足踏波浪，或足踏鱼、蛙，有一种震撼人心的宗教象征意义。所有的一切都保存良好，明亮洁净。

供桌上有些雕刻的小插屏，重点部位有镀金，面部雕刻如牙雕般精致，制作工艺精湛而考究，被妥善地用玻璃罩着。

My desire for a picture in this hall struggled
with my sense of propriety; but finally, after wan-
dering through the hall of five hundred Lohans,
dogged by a priest who was called to talk to the
foreigners because he could say,"Good-bye; Thank
you ; fife lohan". we went back to the main hall and
got permission to make a picture. Dorothy talked
to the priests while I worked, and she put them in
a very friendly mood. One told us what a wonderful
place P'u-T'o is, that here in Yun Lin they have
over a hundred priests, and some more about it. We
left a little silver to have incense burned for us
when we set out to climb to the Monastery of
Secluded Light.

想拍张主殿照片的渴望与合乎礼节的意识挣扎着，最后我们还是在一个只能用英语说"再见""谢谢""五百罗汉"的僧人跟随下，参观了五百罗汉堂。我们回到主殿并得到拍照的许可。我在拍照时，多萝西在和僧人们交谈，他们开始变得友好起来。有位僧人告诉我们，"普陀"是个很好的地方，云林禅寺有一百多位僧人，而普陀的僧人则更多。我们留下了少许银角作为香火钱，然后出发去爬韬光寺。

韬光寺
Tao Guang Temple

韬光寺内的丹涯宝洞
Dan Ya Treasure Cave in Tao Guang Temple

马尔智和多萝西在韬光寺内
Benjamin March and Dorothy were in Tao Guang Temple

On the way up the hill we missed our path at first and had to go back, but soon got on the main road through the bamboo forest, and came to the steps up through the green bamboos to the the orange-walled, black-roofed pavilion that marks the gate of T'ao Kuang. From the porch of this temple we had a glorious view of the wooded valley, the temple below, and the lake in the distance. We drank tea, then climbed up back of the temple to the Pavilion of Refined Elixir and xxxxxxxxxxxxxxxxxxxx the Mystery Cave of the Red Precipice. Here we ate our lunch, and looked at the lake, and rested and recalled that a poem about this place was one of the first in Unity that interested May Johnson in getting me in touch with Dorothy. We and the bamboos whispered together.

上山时，我们一开始走错了路，不得不折回。但穿过竹林，很快就走到主路上，拾级而上，穿过一片翠竹，来到橙墙黑瓦的亭子，便是韬光寺山门。从寺庙的露台望去，可见茂密山谷、下面的寺院和远处西湖的壮丽美景。我们喝完茶，然后爬到寺庙的后面，那儿有吕祖炼丹台和丹崖宝洞。我们在这里吃午餐，看看西湖，歇歇脚，并且想起了我曾经写过的关于此地的一首诗。这是我第一次发表在《团结》杂志上的其中一首诗，梅·约翰逊因此饶有兴趣地为我和多萝西牵线。我们和竹子一起喃喃私语。

On the way down we knoticed that the so-called "golden lotus" were no more than the yellow cow lilies that cluttered up many a lake and pond at home to the sorrow of those who prefered the white water lilies. There are but a few pools of these "choice" flowers in Hangchou, and I must admit, that, common as the are to me, they have a certain charm in a small pool of old moss-covered rocks.

下山时，我们注意到所谓的"金莲"只不过是些黄色的睡莲，在我家乡的湖泊和池塘种了许多，这会让那些喜欢白莲的人感到遗憾。然而在杭州，只有极少数池塘种了这些"精选"的品种。我必须承认，这些对我来说很常见，不过，当它们被种在怪石嶙峋、青苔斑驳的小池塘时，还是别有韵味的。

When we came back through Yun Lin the priests were at afternoon prayers, and the men in their black robes and red outer robes seen against the dimness of the interior through a red doorway, all standing or kneeling or moving in unison, made a picture, accompanied by their chants and drums and bells, that was thrilling to our souls.

当我们回到云林禅寺时，僧人们正在做晚课。透过红色大门，看见他们身着黑衣红褂在昏暗的室内，或站或跪或走动，齐声诵经，构成一幅和谐画面，伴随着缭绕梵音和钟鼓齐鸣声，不断震撼着我们的心灵。

This monastery is quite the most active and apparently best-supported that ı have seen yet in China. It reminds me very strongly of some of the fine ones in Japan, where Buddhism is a real live religion and vital force in the life of the people. Here at Yun Lin there was nothing to support the contention that Buddhism is dead or dying. As to temple, priests, and most of all surroundings I was well pleased to accord this a chief place in my estimations of places of beauty and religious significance in the China I know.

这个寺庙是我们在中国看到的香火最旺的，显然是获得了充足的财力支持。这让我不由地想起日本一些精美的寺庙，在那里，佛教已经与生活融为一体并且焕发出勃勃生机。这里，在云林禅寺，没有什么可支持佛教已经死亡或正在消亡的论点。在我了解的范围内，就寺庙、僧侣和周边的环境而言，我可以很乐观地推断，云林禅寺是中国一处极为迷人、并且有宗教意义的主要寺庙。

From Lin Ying we walked on up a paved road
through a valley lined with small temples belonging
to one general group of the Indias, and with little
villages and groups of houses. We went straight up
to the Monastery of Upper India, a great old place,
now dingy and run-down, with a temple court that
might be beautiful filled with the booths of the
sellers of all sorts of trinkets and souvenirs and
rosaries and bells, not unlike the small dealers
who make such a paltry bazaar of the great shrine
of St. Anne de Beaupre near Quebec. The main hall,
supposedly one of the finest specimens of temple
architecture in Hangchou, is falling to pieces. The
whole place was dis-spiriting. We inquired for some
famous square bamboo trees said to grow here only in
all this area of Hangchou, and were shown them in the
court of a new building evidently built for the en-
tertainment of guests who want to come her and stay
for a little while. The bamboos do not grow to a
great height or to large diameter, and their squarenes
is not apparent to the eye. They are distinctly four-
sided to the touch, however, and they are a little
rough in texture, and dark green in color. The old
priest here was intelligent and pleasant and we talked a bit as we drank tea and ate cakes and nuts.

从灵隐寺出来，我们沿着山谷间的一条石板路往上走，路两旁都是属于天竺寺庙群的小寺庙，还有些小村庄和房子。我们径直走到上天竺，一个曾经宏伟和古老的地方，如今已经破败不堪。寺庙的庭院过去可能有许多漂亮的小店铺，出售各式各样的小饰品、纪念品、念珠或铃铛之类的，肯定不同于魁北克圣安妮教堂小商小贩组成的卑劣集市。主殿也许是杭州寺庙建筑的最好样本之一，如今正变得支离破碎，整个看起来有点让人寒心。我们打听，据说是杭州地区唯一一处、颇负盛名的方竹林。被带到一个新建的院落，显然它是为来这里逗留的游客准备的。这里的方竹长得不高也不粗，人的肉眼难辨方圆，触摸时会有独特的四棱触感，质地有些粗糙，是深绿色的。这里的老和尚睿智而和善，我们闲聊了会儿，喝喝茶，吃吃点心和干果。

上天竺法喜寺
Fa Xi Temple of Shang Tian Zhu

On the way down the valley again we stopped
at the Middle and Lower Temples of India, but we were
not impressed, and passed on. From the main road we
turned off to a side path over the hills before we
reached Lin Ying again. This brought us to a sudden
thunder storm which came up gloriously with one half
of the sky covered with dense black clouds while the
sun shone over them lighting brilliantly the tumbled
white cumulus clouds of the other half, and it also
brought us, soaking wet, to our boat which had gone
around to Mao Chia P'u to meet us. The rain let up
and we started home to chase across the lake a perfect arching rainbow that at one time had one end in
the Three Pools and the other in Heart of the Lake,
but which retreated before us as we approached until
we lost it in the city.

下山途中，我们在中天竺和下天竺逗留片刻，但并未留下什么深刻的印象，
继续赶路。在回到灵隐寺之前，我们避开大路，转而走在旁边的小路上穿过山谷。
突然间雷声大作，一半的天空乌云密布，另一半的天空艳阳高照着不断翻滚的白
色堆积云，我们浑身湿漉漉地回到早已等候在茅家埠的小船。雨停了，我们在回
家的路上追逐完美的彩虹，彩虹的一端已落在三潭印月，另一端落在湖心亭；但
当我们靠近时，彩虹又不断退后，直至消失在城市的上空。

This was avery good day, with many causes for
satisfaction. Hangchou's reputation for beauty might
rest on Lin Ying alone. It is not so appealing as,
for instance, Koyasan, but that place is unique.
Still its very genuine beauty of nature and artifice
cannot be denied, and I, under its charm and spell,
would not deny it if I could. I am glad we saved
this until the last.

这真是美好的一天，有很多因素让我们感到满足。杭州美景的美誉，唯独留给了灵隐。虽然它不如其他地方如高野山（日本）那么吸引人，但它却是独一无二的。它是一种真正的美，既有自然天成，也有人工雕琢之美。不可否认的是，我已被它的神奇魅力深深折服。很高兴，我们终究拥有了这段经历。

给马尔智夫妇划船的态度十分友善的西湖船工
A boatman on West Lake who was friendly and rowed a boat for Benjamin March and his wife

马尔智在西湖游船上
Benjamin March was on a pleasure boat on West Lake

We took aur small boat this morning, with the girl instead of the man at the paddle, and made our way around the lake.　About noon we stopped at the quiet little Temple of the White Cloud　we had visited before, and herewe spent a couple hours in writing and reading and eating our lunch and just enjoying the fellwoship of each other and beauty and quiet. Then we went on, through the Inner Lake and the lagoons, andunder bridges, and in and out. We stopped at several places of which I wanted to get pictures, loafed under a very old bridge, and finally came home back of Imperial Island, past the Pavilion from which the Storks were Sent Forth,and the last part of the trip raced an oncoming storm. The black clouds filled the west and the white sheet of rain moved down the valley out toward the Imperial Island and us. The man, who had returned but shortly äefore rushed out to meet us and helped to hurry us to shore.　(Since the very first we have always used this man with his boat, or the girl with hers(they belong together) and they know us well now.)　We hiked along up to our house and got up on our porch in time to see the storm catch us, and a mighty storm of wind and rain it was, well fulfilling its majestic promise. Wwe were home early, so had time to read some, to play the piano some, and to amuse ourselves a little befere and after supper and before we went to bed to get a good cool sleep.

今天早上，我们乘着小船环湖，划船的是那个船娘而不是船夫。大约中午时分，我们来到以前游览过的宁静小寺——白云庵。在这里度过了两个小时，写作、阅读和午餐时间，只是享受着彼此相伴的安宁与美好。然后接着上船，穿过内湖，在桥下来回穿梭。我们在我想拍照的几个地方稍作停留。小船悠然穿过一座老桥，便来到了御岛（孤山），经过放鹤亭，游览的最后部分，是与即将来临的暴雨争渡。乌云密布了西边的天空，白色雨幕倾泻山间，正朝孤山和我们袭来。比我们早到一步的船夫很快冲出来接我们，急急忙忙地拉我们上岸（从第一次开始我们就一直雇佣这个船夫和船，或者和他一起的船娘，现在他们和我们很熟）。我们徒步赶回住处，刚上凉台，风雨交加的暴雨便如期而至。回家比较早，所以有时间读了会书，又弹了会钢琴。餐前餐后、临睡前，我们都自娱自乐了一番，之后便甜甜睡去。

马尔智在白云庵花园内留影
Benjamin March's photo taken as
a memento in the garden of white
Cloud Nunnery

马尔智夫人多萝西在白云庵花园内留影
Dorothy's photo (Benjamin
March' wife) taken as a memento in
the garden of White Cloud Nunnery

Before going on with Monday it is highly proper
than on the first day of the week I recount our
adventures of Sabbath night.   One afternoon in
strolling through the town we passed what looked
like a movie show, and Sunday night we were in a
mood to investigate it. We went out early in the
evening, and paid our couple dimes for admission
to the place where the movies signs were. We found
ourselves in an open court, where was a stage, and
many tables, but in which were no men, for the
weather was not auspicious. Instead of staying in
the pleasant open court men, mostly young men, and
quite a few girls, many of the latter with the men,
hurried across the court to the Buildings, two or
more stories in height, which surrounded it. In
one of these was a theater, and large house built
in the western manner, but playing Chinese plays.
The audience came and went easily, and the play
progressed, though it was poor acting by a poor
company. We left the crowded hall and passed another smaller hall, filled with tables like the
usual Chinese theater. Another poor actor was giving a solo in the manner that has become the con-
ventional representation of a woman on the Chinese
stage. We went upstairs, and past a kind of restaurant or refreshment parlor where two girls were
playing and singing. We went up another flight to

　　另一周随着周一即将开启前，我应当先叙述下我们在安息日晚上的冒险。某个下午，我们在城里闲逛，看到一处像是电影院的地方，周日晚我们心情不错，打算去一探究竟。我们早早就出发了，付了几角钱进了挂有标识的电影院。我们发现自己置身于一个露天的院子，有个戏台，还摆了许多桌子。由于天气不太好，并没有人入座。来这里的大多是年轻男子，也有为数不多的女孩，大多都有男伴。他们并没有选择开阔舒适的院子，匆匆穿过院子，走进四周二层或更高的楼里，其中之一是个戏院，很大，建筑风格是西洋式的，正在上演着中国戏剧。观众进出自如，演出依然在继续，尽管只是一个草台班子低水平的演出。我们离开拥挤的大厅，穿过一个摆满了桌子的小厅，就像中国剧院常见的那样。一个蹩脚的旦角正在台上独自表演，是那种在中国舞台上颇具代表性的女性形象。我们上了二楼，经过一个餐厅亦或是客厅，两个女子正在那儿弹唱。

a roof where a movie show as in progress. Here were
ancient French films wretchedly projected to an
audience that seemed to enjoy the darkness. Coming
down we stopped for a minute where a company of
actors who looked like students were giving modern
plays in the modern, that is the western manner.
Near the outside door wasa pool hall, and there were
indications of other halls and other amusements in
farther halls. It was a pitiful place, for none
of the entertainments were first class, the place
itself was tawdry, the audience mostly young men,
students and some older men, all looking for something of a good time that was not here. It was a
Coney Island without the American flare for convin-
cing them. It was akin to the New World and such
places in Peking and other large cities. While it
is no worse herethan the same thing at home, one
cannot but wonder what it signifies in the changing
life of the nation.

　　我们又上了一层楼，来到顶楼，这里正放映电影。这是一部法国老电影，虽
然影片放映质量很差，但观众似乎很享受这种黑暗的氛围。下楼我们逗留片刻，
一家看似是学生剧团正以现代方式，或者说是西方方式，在演出现代剧。大门口
就是一个台球房，这四周其他小楼应该还有很多娱乐场所和项目。这是个不入流
的地方，没有一个娱乐项目是一流的，看起来艳俗廉价。观众大多是年轻人、学
生，还有一些年长的男人，此处并没有他们所追寻的美好时光。这里就像纽约的
康尼岛，只不过是没有美国式装模作样的张扬而已。在北京及其他大城市，都有
类似的"新世界"，美国也好不到哪里去，人们不禁要问，民众生活的如此变化究
竟意味着什么？

Monday we stayed at home all day. We had planned to go out in the afternoon, but as the afternoon came there came with it a storm of rain, and we stayed on our porch, drinking tea and reading Marco Polo. We also began toddy the construction of a cook book. Dorothy has long wondered how she might legitimately use the several colored paper with which I fill my pocket notebook and keep various kinds of notes. She decided that a looseleaf cook book, arranged like my note systems so t that the sheets can be kept in a book binder or filed in a drawer would provide the excuse. Consequently I started typing recipes out of magazines using pink paper for desserts, beverages and the l like; blue for vegetables; yellow for meats, soups, gravies, etc.; and white for pastry, breadstuffs, and general directions. Quite a gay cook book should result.

周一我们在家里呆了一整天。原本计划下午出门，不料午后一场雷阵雨来袭，我们只好呆在门廊里，边喝茶边阅读《马可·波罗（游记）》。今天我们开始着手编一本菜谱。多萝西很早就在琢磨如何合理地使用我口袋笔记本里的那些彩色纸张，作不同类型的笔记。最后她决定做一本活页菜谱，排列次序如我的笔记系统，这样笔记就可以夹在书夹中或是放在抽屉里归档。因此，我开始照着杂志上的菜单打印整理。粉红色纸张，打印的是甜点和饮品一类；蓝色纸张，打印的是素菜类；黄色上打印的是肉类、汤类和肉汁等的做法；白色的是糕点、面包和烹调基本常识。这会是一本色彩鲜艳的烹饪食谱。

Having long had some pictures on my mind
that required the morning light for their making
we hiked out this morning to the end of the old
city wall, and from there got an excellent view of
the Needle Pagoda, without the insulting Main house.

　　长久以来，有些需要在晨曦中拍出来的画面，一直萦绕在我的脑海里。今晨，我们便登上古老城墙的末段。在这里我们找到一个拍摄保俶塔的绝佳角度，可以避开梅恩那幢丑陋的建筑。

In the afternoon we wandered into the town again, and went to the fan shop to get one or two new papers, and another fan for a gift. It is a fascinating place from which we can hardly stay long away. On the way we stopped at a shop to get some cloth for a new hiking blouse Dorothy planned to make for herself, and while there saw and got some very pretty stuff for a summer dress for next summer, stuff distinctive to Hangzhou. We poked around a while longer, and then returned to our house, where we had supper. After supper I developed four rolls of film, which pleased us much with their good pictures. I should say we developed, for I worked by time in a dark room, and Dorothy held the clock outside. We are making quite a success of this cooperative photography.

下午，我们又逛进城里，去扇店买了一两个扇面和另外一把作为礼物的扇子，这里真是一个难以割舍的地方。我们还在一家布店驻足，多萝西要为自己选购用来制作一件远足上衣的布料，在店里又看到一些很漂亮又很有杭州特色的布料，于是下单，准备来年夏天做裙子。我们又闲逛了一会儿，然后回家吃晚饭。饭后，我冲印了四个胶卷，看到这些好照片真令人高兴。应该说是我们两人共同完成的，我在暗房里冲洗时，多萝西在外面计时。这次摄影合作非常成功。

I woke up this morning as the sun was just spreading out his cool bright fingers over the city and the surrounding country, touching and polishing the Needle Pagoda with one long forefinger, and making the city clean before men should be well abroad with their genius to befoul it again before night-fall. The beauty of the cool cloudless morning tempted me from my bed and I rose, to write a little indifferent verse which pleased me much.

今晨醒来，太阳正将它那清丽明快的手，舒展向这座城市和乡村，食指碰触并摩挲着保俶塔，人们即将出门一展其污秽之能事直至天黑，它要赶在他们之前把整个城市捯饬干净。被清朗明媚的晨光所感染，我起床赋闲诗一首，心生愉悦。

In the early afternoon, immediately after lunch, we took rickshas and rode out of the city, through narrow streets, and along a white and green canal, to the Six Harmony Pagoda. I had been wanting to visit it again, and to try a couple pictures I had not been able to make succeed the last time. Today we went again, and again we climbed to the top. In the clear sunlight of early afternoon we could see out over the country, to the far blue hills and the distant waters of the bay into which the pirates used to come to terrorize the city. A brisk wind drove the laden junks up the green Ch'ien T'ang river We loafed and enjoyed the scene, then bumped back over the rough paved streets to town and home.

午后不久，我们一用完午餐，便坐人力车出城，穿过狭窄的街道，沿着清澈的运河，奔向六和塔。我一直想再去游览六和塔，并拍些照片，上次拍的不是很成功。今日故地重游，再次爬上塔顶。在午后明媚的阳光下，乡村一览无余，远处苍翠的青山掩映着江湾，海盗们曾在此登陆，威胁着杭州城。微风吹过助力钱塘江上的货船逆流而上。我们悠闲地享受着美好时光，之后又一路颠簸回城并回到家。

杭州城内的一条运河
A canal in Hangzhou city

西湖边的亭台楼榭
Pavilions, platforms, Chambers and towers on the side of West Lake

When we had returned and refreshed ourselves we took our supper down to our boat and went out on the lake to enjoy the moon, rapidly nearing its time of fullness for the month. We drifted and paddled about the lake and the islands. After supper we sat, wrote a little verse, and then Dorothy sang for a long while and I lay on my back watching the white moon. A good day, a very good day - and no rain.

回来休整片刻，我们带着晚餐，泛舟湖上赏月，月亮几近盈满。我们划行飘浮于湖岛间。饭后，我们坐在小船上，作了首小诗，多萝西吟唱了许久，我躺在船上仰望着白色月光。今日无雨，再美好不过的一天。

This day is our first "mooniversary! We have been married one month, and are well pleased. This day also is another bright clear cloudless day, with a fine cooling wind, a paradisial day. We had the cook make us some good Chinese food for lunch, and immediately after eating it we got rickshas and rode out along the motor road to visit Ling Yin, the Spirits' Retreat again. Here we loitered along, made some more pictures of the place, then wandered into the great hall of the monastery, and sat down to talk to the priests and commune with the gods.

(Here I turn the Memoirs over to Dorothy.)

今天是我们的第一个"满月"。结婚的这一个月，我们都甚感愉悦。今天依旧是阳光明媚、晴空万里的一天，清风送爽，天堂般的好日子。中午，厨师给我们做了顿丰盛的中餐，吃完后，我们立即乘坐人力车，沿着机动车道又去了灵隐—— 心灵归隐之地。我们在寺庙里逛了很久，拍了许多照片，然后走进大雄宝殿，坐下来和僧人们聊天，参禅礼佛。

（这里，我将日记移交多萝西来写）

灵隐寺大雄宝殿
Mahavira Hall (Daxiong Bao Dian) in Lingyin Temple

大雄宝殿内的如来佛
Tathagata in Mahavira Hall (Daxiong Bao Dian)

"A wisp of sunlight, strayed from the western glory, crept into the Temple of the Spirits' Rest, and caught on the peaceful fingers of the Blessed One, at rest in the heart of the Lotus -

"Suddenly the jovial, short-coated priest who had been joking and laughing stopped, and looking at the sunlight said,

"' It is the hour.'

"He moved with a briskness that contrasted strangely with the quiet of the great temple where a silent bell, a silent crimson drum, the wistful wreaths of smoke from fragrant incense and the three great golden images were patient and still.

夕阳西斜，一缕余晖悄悄洒在佛陀那平和的指尖。此时，佛陀在灵隐寺大殿的莲花座上休憩。

穿着短衫的僧人原本正开心说笑，突然停了下来，看着这缕余晖说道："是时候了。"

他行动敏捷，与宁静大殿中沉寂的大钟、无声的绯红色鼓、袅袅的青烟、静默的三尊金色大佛（西方三圣），形成鲜明的对比。

"It is the hour,' he called, and another grey
robed figure came to help him prepare the lofty
temple for the evening vespers.

"The great lamp of amber oil that burns before Gotama was slowly lowered and a new wick lit.
The flame was garnet and the Buddha's eyes were
glad when it was raised until it brightened the
blue jewel in his forehead.

"The great bell was struck three times, and
slow sighing tones rose among the red pillars and
joined the mourning of white pigeons in the rafters
                                              hot
"Chips of sandalwood were lit in the ashes of
incense. Red candles lit the gilded tables of
sacrifice.

"The priests did not speak. They hurried as
if this were a welcome break in the monotony of the
day.

"到点了！"他喊道，一个穿灰袍的僧人过来，帮他一起在高耸的大殿里准备做晚课。

他们徐徐降下在释迦牟尼前燃烧的巨大琥珀油灯，点亮一根新的灯芯。当油灯升起直至石榴色的火焰，照亮了佛祖头上的蓝宝石，佛祖眼带笑意。

大钟敲响三下，悠扬的钟声和着椽子上白鸽的咕咕声，在红色的柱子间回荡。

热香灰中的檀香片和那镀金供桌上的红蜡烛被一一点燃。

僧人之间并无交流，只是忙碌着，就好像把他们从单调的一天中解脱出来了。

"A bowl of paper money was prepared, to ascend
in quick flames for the honor of the Blessed One,
and palm leaf fans were placed in piles on the two
side offering boxes.

"The two priests kicked the brown fiber hass-
socks into line as they went to put on their long
robes.

"A far bell in a side court sounded, again,
again. The priest who acted as monitor for the day's
vespers came in and bowed until his smooth head was
pressed against the harsh fiber stool. Then, from
each side, through tall doors, priests came, their
hands folded, their eyes lowered, and over their
shoulders the Robes of Renunciation, brown ones,
tan ones, black and yellow, purple and grey; and
the priests stood waiting until the Abbot xxxxxxx
xxxxxxxx came.

他们把准备好的一碗纸钱扔进大火中以供奉佛祖，并在两侧的功德箱放了一
堆棕榈扇。

两个僧人将棕色蒲团摆成一行，然后穿上了长袈裟。

旁边院子的钟声一次次响起，当晚值班僧侣走进来，并虔诚地跪下，他的光
头叩拜在毛糙的蒲团上。接着，其他僧人从每个侧门，穿过高高的殿门，鱼贯而
入。他们肩披各色袈裟，有棕色、褐色、黄黑色、紫灰色。他们双手合十，眼睛
低垂，齐齐站立，恭候住持的到来。

"His robe was scarlet, and the central hassock, the large blue-covered round one with its special prayer cloth, was his.

"The crimson drum sounded, a tinkling bell and a bronze bell rang, one voice rose in the minor music of the First Song of Praise to the One in the Heart of the Lotus, and all the voices joined it - slowly, deep tones from old men, and shrill, quicker pipings from those with children's faces.

"The fragrance of the sandalwood lifted from the bronze censer.

"The lonely wisp of sunlight wavered and went out again to lose itself in the beauty of the sunset beyond the valley of the Spirits' Rest."

　　住持身披深红色的袈裟，他的蒲团在正中，大大的，用专供跪拜的蓝色布料包裹着。

　　鼓声阵阵，钟磬悠扬，一个声音响起，低声歌颂着莲花座上的佛陀，所有的声音随后加入——长者的声音低缓深沉，面带稚气的小僧声音尖锐急促。

　　檀香的芬芳从铜炉中飘出。

　　这缕孤独的余晖逐渐暗淡，随着美丽的落日，一同消失在灵隐山谷中。

The service lasted for a full hour with its chanting, its processionals, and its ceremony. The abbot, a man not recently shaven, with the expression of a professional religionist, one whose business it is to be resigned and meek and whose mouth was carefully tucked in at the corners to show it, led most of the service, or at least took the central part. A young priest performed the more active ceremonies, the devotions before the images, the blessing of a cup of oil and the pouring of it in the proper receptacle outside. He seemed like a lad quick to learn, though not gifted with high prowess for his own part. These two alone had the special black-bordered prayer cloths with the red squares in the corners.

这堂晚课从诵经、行进到行佛礼，整整持续了一个小时。那位早已剃度的住持一举一动，都表现出了一个职业僧人的操守。他面色虔诚，嘴唇微动，心无旁骛地轻声诵吟着佛经，仪式中的大部分环节至少是其中最关键的环节都由他引领。一个年轻的僧人，承担了其中更为动态的仪式。在佛像前跪拜，为一杯香油施福并将其倒入门外的容器中。他天资不高，但似乎很善于学习。只有他和住持，穿着四周带红色方块、特殊黑边的僧袍。

The monitor was thin and devout, and wore the look and manner of a general. It was he who order- ed the positions of the monks, and he who set half a dozen at work walking up and down the lines fanning the others. There were about fifty men, all told. The monitor is the sort of man who leads movements and establishes sects, though if his would be any contribution to the spirit I doubt.

当班僧人清瘦而虔诚，仪表及举止，就是一般僧人的模样。他调整了众僧的队列，派了五六个僧人来回走动，为其他僧人扇风。大殿里约有 50 个僧人。当班僧人负责引领礼佛活动，确立宗派体系。但他的行为对佛教精神的贡献到底有多大，我还是有些怀疑。

Most of the men justify the low opinion of the monastic fellowship. There were young men, lads with sullen or greedy faces, or indifferent. There were middle aged men, some with the appearance of those who enjoy the idleness of the monastery, a few looking as though the monastery had provided them with a refuge, adn escape. There were old men who had grown flabby in the ranks, smirking and mechanically going through the formulae. There were men like the jovial friendly priest who had talked with us who acted as if not quite sure why they were there; men depressed by idleness at the same time that they enjoyed it, men, perhaps, dedicated in their childhood to the temple's service. Who knows the stories behind the grey robes?

大多数人对寺院僧侣持有成见。也难怪，看着这些出家人，就能理解为什么他们的名声不太好了。年轻僧人的面色，或阴沉，或贪婪，或冷漠。中年僧人则看起来很享受寺院的闲散，有几个看起来已经把这里当成了避世的收容所。年长的僧人，疲沓地微笑着跟着队伍，机械地行进。有些僧人看起来和刚才与我们谈话的僧人一样虽和颜悦色，但似乎并不十分确定自己为什么会出家。或许他们是在很小的时候就被送进寺院，生活虽令人沮丧，但他们却还是很享受。又有谁知道这些灰色僧袍背后的故事呢？

And there was one priest. He stood tall and pale the second from the end of the first line. White clean cuffs of his under coat showed below the sleeves of his black robe. Long slim hands clasped and unclasped themselves in prayer, and intermittenly wiped the perspiration from his blue and gleaming freshly shaven head. Long ears, and fine face, eyes that could see more worlds than one, - here was a man known to the spirit. Here was a man who made the traditions of great scholarly priests and great prophets live in my mind. Here was a man who might, under proper environment become the great painter that some priest have been, who might write a new and consummate revelation of faith, who give men new visions. No religion could be wholly dead or without hope that could produce, or attract, or hold such a man. Here in a living man seemed to be incarnate the sweet calm, the loving tolerance, and the peaceful meditativeness of ideal Buddhism. It was more than worth andfternoon to have seen such an one.

　　第一排倒数第二位个子高高、面色苍白的僧人，穿着黑色的僧袍里，露出白色内衣干净的袖子。念经时，他那纤长的双手时开时合，不时抬手去擦刚剃过的青亮头皮上的汗水。他是一位很有佛性的僧人，长长的耳朵，面容和善，双眼对世间的洞察胜于他人。他精通佛学，就像我心目中的高僧大德一样。假以时日，这位僧人也会像其他很多僧人那样成为伟大的画家，也许还会写出新的完美的佛家经典，给人指引新的境界。能孕育、吸收或拥有这样的信徒，信仰就有了生机，不会消亡。这位僧人仿佛是佛教理想的、甜蜜安定的化身，有着宽容的爱心和平和的心境。能看到这样的僧人，下午才不虚此行。

We waited quietly until all was over. The
antiphonal chanting, the responses, the processionals; until the priests had filed out and gone to
their several quarters; then we left the now dim
hall where the tall pillars were made of American
pines from Oregon and where Buddha sat in peace.
We came back to Imperial Island, and went into a
well-known restaurant for a mooniversary spree.
We were early, and got a pleasant table on the bal-
cony overlooking the lake. We ate fish, little
puffy rolls (though bearing that name only because
they are rolled and I know no better in English),
young lotus beades boiled with ham, vermicelli with
fresh shrimps and young bamboo, a little wine, and
tea. It was very excellent dinner, featuring
several Hangchou specialities.

The moon was high in the sky as we walked home
in the darkening evening.

僧人们轮流念诵、应和、行进，直到他们陆续退出回到自己的僧舍。我们静
静地守候着，直到晚课结束。之后，我们离开昏暗的大殿，殿内的高大柱子是由
来自于美国俄勒冈州的松木做成的，佛祖平和地端坐着。我们回到了孤山，走进
一家颇负盛名的餐馆（楼外楼）庆祝我们的新婚满月。因为去得早，得以坐在可俯
瞰西湖的阳台上用餐。我们吃了鱼、蓬松小卷（予以此名，只因其是个卷，找不
出更好的英语表达）、火方蒸嫩藕、鲜虾笋尖烩粉丝，还喝了点葡萄酒和茶。点了
几道杭州的特色菜，晚餐棒极了。

夜色阑珊，明月当空伴着我们归家。

This was another rare day, and in the afternoon we went into the city and found our way up to the top of the temple-lined hill near the south end of the inclosure. Here we saw the characteristically Taoist and rather squalid Tung Yuen Miao (Temple of the Sacred Mountain of the East) and the City Temple, the Ch'eng Huang Miao. Poking along the ridge from temple to temple we came to a small one, whose well kempt appearance and attractive stage enticed us to enter. Several scholarly looking men were at tables with books and writing equipment. They bowed us welcomeas we enetered. Within the hall were three gods, attended each by two demons. The central one appeared to be himself a demon, for his face was sharp, his eyes and hair were red, and he wore only leaves for a dress. He was the god of medicine one of the men explained to us, and this temple was maintained by the doctors of the city. It had not preisthood and belonged to no religion, but the doctors came here and prayed before performing operations, then sat here and studied their books under the guidance of the deity, who taught them w where to cut, and gave their hands skill. Of the temples we visited none was more interesting than this, which was not listed in our guide books

今天又是个难得的好日子。下午我们进了城，爬上了城南一座寺庙林立的小山（吴山）。我们参观了典型的道观——破败的东岳庙（供奉的是东岳大帝即泰山神），还有保佑杭州城的城隍庙。沿着山脊线，寺庙一座一座，我们来到一个小庙，保存完好的外观及引人注目的戏台，吸引着我们走进。几个学者模样的人坐在桌旁，桌上放着书和文房四宝。看到我们进来，赶紧起身相迎。庙内供奉着三神，每个神仙旁都立着两个小鬼，中间的那个似乎是恶魔，长着一张魔鬼似的脸，红发红眼，树叶当衣。庙里的人解释说这是药神。庙宇是由城里的医生集资筹建的，没有僧职，不属任何教派。医生在动手术前，都会到这里朝拜，按照神的旨意在此研究医书，药神教给他们手术的部位并赐予他们手术技能。导游手册上并未标注此处，但这确实是我们游历过的最有趣的寺庙了。

Some of the temples were filled with soldiers whose manners as we passed were not always of the finest. We attempted to enter none of these. We went on to the top of the hill, the highest point within the wall, and from there saw the whole town. Here are stones laid in the pattern of k'an, water, the northern of the eight diagrams from which Chinese writing is supposed to have been derived, and which are used in geomancy, in the hope that this will prevent or put out fires . It it ☵. From this height the city looked like a great area of spotted black and white, white walls, marked by black roofs, straight black ridges and black tops of fire walls. Here and there the turrets and domes of modern business establishments and hotels gave a curious touch to the plain. The hill we were on was of rock, with grassy lawns, rock of the type carried away to be placed in gardens, and evidently this had been a garden spot at some time.

路过的一些寺庙里，满是不甚和气的武将，我们都尽量避开。上到山顶，登上城墙内的最高点，这里可以看到整个城市。山顶上有堆石头，堆成了八卦中坎卦的图形。八卦通常用来占卜，据说中国的文字也由八卦演变而来，坎卦属水，位居北方，有生水、防火、消灾之意。这就是☵（坎卦）。从这个高度看整个城市，像是由黑白二色组成，白墙黑瓦，黑色的挺直屋脊，防火墙的黑顶。随处可见的现代商业建筑和旅馆的塔楼及圆顶，显得很突兀。我们所处的山头有很多岩石，还有草坪。这种岩石搬来是布置花园的，很显然，这里曾经是一座花园。

正在建造中的财神庙
God of Wealth Temple Being built

财神庙正殿
Main Hall of God of Wealth Eemple

杭州的一个石牌坊
A memorial stone archway of Hangzhou

一个寺庙大门处的经墙
A red wall near the gate of a temple

杭州古戏台
An ancient opera platform of Hangzhou

After a morning of picking up odds and ends
and puttering around we went out to Hangchou
Christian College, on a beautiful high site by the
river, to see Arthur March. He had called on us
Friday, having heard from some peopel in a nearby
resort where he was with his family, that we were
down here. We decided that we are cousins, though
several generations removed, and we had much sport
speculating on the exact connections. we found
maay points of common interest and opinion. After
a good dinner out on the cool lawn in the moonlight,
just the three ofnus, we went up to the observator y
and looked at moon and satrs until it was high time
for us to be staeting back. It is pleasant to meet
a member of one's family and to enjoy the meeting.
The ride back by moonlight, after the glorious view
of the river from the hilltop,was inspiring.

　　一上午在家中收拾了零星杂物，又闲逛了一小会儿，然后我们出发前往坐落在美丽江边高地的基督教大学（即之江大学），看望亚瑟·马尔智。他和家人在附近度假时听人说起我们也在杭州，便在周五晚拜访了我们。我们的家族关系要上溯好几代，还是决定以堂兄弟相称。我们彼此之间，有着共同的兴趣爱好和见解。月色下，我们仨在户外的草坪上美美地享用了一顿晚餐。之后便一道去天文台观测星星和月亮，直到尽兴才离开。这是一次令人愉快的亲友会面。趁着月色，我们骑马回家，从山巅上望去，身后大江的壮丽景色令人赞叹。

        The whole day we have been out on the lake,
paddling around and revisiting places we have liked.
Tomorrow we leave here for Shanghai.

　　一整天我们都在湖上泛舟，重游那些我们喜爱的地方。明天我们就要离开这里，动身去上海了。

Last night we had been asleep but a short time when we were awakened, about midnight, by what I at first took to be fire works from the sound of explosions and the leaping of flames up into the moonlit night. Soon, however, I became perfectly aware that it was a house on fire, and that the exploding was burning bamboo. The place was just west of our compound across the canal and street, and consequently, as we sat up in bed facing it we had a gorgeous view of the spectacle. And it was a spectacle. The flames shot up through the house and roof and second floor were soon gone. A pillar of smoke rolled off into the air and bits of burning fabric dropped to our lawn and the street. Fortunately all the roofs here are of tin or tile. Crowds began to gather, of course, and the shrill screeching of police whistals that first awakened us kept up for a long time. Drums and cymbals were heard and men with lanterns and torches were soon seen around the burning building, and we knew that efforts were being made to exercise the fire demons. Soon, however, there was another sound, and presently we observed streams of water playing on the standing walls and into the flaming courtyard. I dressed and went down.

昨晚我们没睡多久就被吵醒了，大约在午夜时分，伴随着爆炸声，窜起的火焰照亮了夜空，起初我以为是谁家在放焰火，随后便意识到是谁家着火了。被烧着的竹子发出噼噼啪啪的爆炸声，着火的房子就在我们的西面，隔着一条小河和一条街道。我们坐在床上，便能目击那壮观场面，熊熊烈火直冲而上，二楼和房顶很快烧光，一根冒着浓烟的柱子倒塌，一些易燃的织物飘到我们的草坪和街道上。幸好这里所有的屋顶都是铁片或瓦片。人群开始聚集，最早惊醒我们的刺耳的警笛声持续了很久。很快人们举着火把或灯笼，聚在失火的房子周围，敲锣打鼓驱赶火魔。不久，又传来另一种声音，我们注意到一股股水柱穿过未坍塌的墙体注入着火的院内。我披衣走了下来。

The crowd was a large one, and though some drumming was audible I could not localize it. On the contrary the place was well policed, and even a squad of troops had been turned out. The crowd was quietly observing the fire, and staying back of the police lines so that the fire engines had a chance to work. These were hand pumps, manned by sixteen men each, and drew their water from the canal. I counted eight, and believe there were others I did not notice. The firemen wore metal helmets and presented a queer sight with their shining headgear and their shining bare sweat-wetted backs. They were bravely and systematically doing their work and the fire was well under control though the entire place had been burnt out. I have much respect for the way in which this matter was handled.

一大帮拥挤的人群中，鼓声依稀，难辨方向。反倒是现场已戒备森严，一小支军队也赶到了。人群站在警戒线之后，静静地观察着火势，以便消防车能进去灭火。消防队员每十六人一个手动水泵，从运河里抽水。我数了数有八个水泵，应该还有我没注意到的。消防队员带着金属头盔，打着赤膊，头盔和后背的汗水，在火光下闪闪发光，分外奇特。他们勇敢并有条不紊地工作着，火势很快得到了控制，只是整个院子已经完全被烧光了。整件事情的处理方式令我钦佩。

The building was a dying establishment, where
the common blue and white stenciled goods is made.
Just that morning we had seen hundreds of yards
of the stuff drying on the lawn by the canal. The
place included a large courtyard, with many racks
for hanging the goods, and a long two story house.
It was clear of other buildings on three sides,
and separated by a characteristic high fire wall
from the courts on the fourth. Nothing but the
walls were left after the fire had died down.

失火的是一家快破产的工厂，生产普通的蓝白印花布。早上，我们还看到沿着运河边的草坪上，晾晒着数百码的物品。工厂有个很大的院子，有很多用来垂挂物品的支架，还有一长排二层的楼房。很显然，三面也还有一些其他建筑物。一道很有特色的高高防火墙，与这一面的院子隔开。火灾过后，除了这道防火墙，什么都没有了。

This morning when we started for the train at six-thirty we saw many people carrying away partially burned pieces of timber, and pieces of burned cloth littered the street.

We left Hangchou with regret, and arrived in Shanghai about noon. In the afternoon we set out to do some errands, and did everything we could, though the fact of a bank holiday and the closing of many stores for the afternoon made us hold over some things until the next morning. It it pleasant to shop in regular stores of the home-side variety occasionally, and to sit in a proper candy shop and drink ice cream sodas and buy real chocolates. In the evening we took a long rick-sha ride, ending at the Majestic Lawn Cinema, where we sat in comfortable chairs on a moonlit lawn and watched Strongheart, the famous actor dog, go thru a play that had little besides him to recommend it.

今早六点半，我们出发赶火车时，看到街上很多人在捡拾残留的木板和布片。

我们依依不舍地离开了杭州，中午时分抵达上海。下午，出门办了些能办的事。由于恰逢银行休息日，许多商店下午也未营业，有些事情只能等到明天上午来办。偶尔在普通商场购买本地特产，坐在一家地道甜品店喝冰淇淋苏打水，还买到了正宗的巧克力，真开心。晚上，黄包车拉着我们花了很长时间来到大华饭店屋顶花园影戏场。月色下，草坪上，我们坐在舒适的椅子里，观看了一部由名叫"强心"的明星狗主演的影片。这部电影除明星狗之外，几乎没啥可推荐的了。

We were up betimes this morning, after a
very pure night on two very poor beds. We had been
told that the train left at seven-thirty, but my
love of being early to such performances got us
there before seven, when it actually did go. We
were soon in Soochow and got rickshas to help us
see the town. What could be better for a honeymoon, which is veritably heaven itself, than Hangchou and Soochou, which, the proverb tells us, are
the nearest counterparts to heaven on earth?

昨晚，我们分开睡在了两张破旧的床上，一早便起床了。事先我们听说去苏州的火车 7:30 开，我喜欢赶早，7:00 之前就到了车站，恰巧火车就是 7:00 出发，我们便很快到了苏州。黄包车拉着我们观看市容市貌。俗话说得好："上有天堂，下有苏杭。"还有什么地方能比杭州、苏州这些简直就是天堂的地方更适合度蜜月呢？

西湖断桥
Broken Bridge of Hangzhou